Authenticity in Chaos

Written by

Sean Patrick Toal

Table of Contents

Who am I?

My name is Sean Toal, and I was born in 1985 to a loving family of hard-working people with traditional catholic values. I was raised a catholic, attended chapel regularly as a youngster, and studied in both a catholic primary and secondary school. During my time in school, I was told that I was academically switched on but lacked interest in many of the subjects being taught to me, which probably didn't help my already poor attention span. As a teenager, I probably saw myself as a type of *'jack the lad'* figure who liked clubbing at the weekends and would rather party than knuckle down and commit to either football or any other subject that would have benefited me in the long run. I was so impressed with materialistic stuff, such as designer clothes, money, nice cars, and everything else that impresses a young teenager. I went to college to study sports coaching, which I loved, but I was unable to finish the HND course because of the tragic situation that changed my life forever at the young age of 19.

At the age of 19, whilst drinking and having a good time at my ex-girlfriend's house, a fight broke out over a girl who had been seeing my friend whilst in another relationship, which resulted in a young man losing his life. I was convicted of murder after this fight and served 15 years for a crime I did not commit. This book is not about my case; that will be for another time, but this horrific event devastated so many lives, including the victim's family who suffered unimaginable loss, alongside my own family and other families close to the case, causing deep wounds that will never heal for some people. I am in no way trying to make myself look like an angel, but I was certainly not a career criminal by any means, and this very serious crime was my one and only conviction.

Authenticity in chaos

This event was life-changing for me, to say the least, and set me up for a life of unauthentic behaviors, attitudes, emotions, ego, feelings, etc., and literally changed my whole identity. At the age of 19, I entered the Scottish Prison System. This was so alien to me, and it is hard to express the difference in environments and the unnatural feelings and emotions that this caused. I spent 15 years in the prison system learning how to survive in a dangerous and toxic setting where many social norms and socially acceptable behaviors are reversed. An example would be the acceptance and, in many ways, celebrated acts of violence which occur whilst in prison. These acts of violence would be seen as unacceptable and anti-social in society, but in the micro sub-society of prison, these acts of violence become normal and totally acceptable within prisoner values and norms set in this rough terrain.

One thing society and prison have in common for the most part is the normality in our society and the sub-society of prison to want nice things, and many people inside and out believe success to be how much money someone has managed to attain or how successful other people believe you are. As a society, we care so much about what people think of us and what people think of our family, etc. This can cause major conflict within and can cause people to either believe they are not good enough or give us a distorted view of ourselves, where we think we are not good enough for some reason. Many of us have a feeling of emptiness that we cannot explain and do not really explore the reason we feel 'like' this, but I believe this to be the disconnection from our true, authentic selves.

"Sometimes the emptiness is just a reminder that there's space for something new."

- Terri Guillemets

2

If you're someone who is genuinely content with themselves and lives as their authentic self, then you're among the exceptions, and you've done well in mastering life. I, on the other hand, am still a humble student on the path to discovering my true self. I fall into the traps of social norms frequently, with social media being perhaps the most insidious one.

I see myself at times comparing my life to someone else's unauthentic life, which they are projecting on the world as problem-free and amazing; the saddest part is, I know that this is a projection of fake positivity, but I am so deeply conditioned I still need to make the comparison. I honestly believe many of us are addicted to social media, and in some way, this is entangled with a paradoxical addiction to stress:

"All the suffering, stress, and addiction comes from not realizing you already are what you are looking for."

- Jon Kabat-Zinn

The world's richest man, Elon Musk, the owner of one of the biggest social media platforms (Twitter), has continually warned of the dangers of the unauthentic world of social media:

"I think there should be regulations on social media to the degree that it affects the public good."

- Elon Musk

I have used the platform of social media as an example of when we actually know we are being unauthentic but portray the illusion that this is our authentic self; this is, in fact, what we want others to believe is our actual life, and unknowingly we are actually being the opposite to our true self as we have been conditioned by society to hide our true authentic self.

'Authenticity' is a deep and thought-provoking subject, which has many differing views and opinions; however, the point I set out to make with social media is if we cannot be our authentic selves in society, what chance do we have in a prison environment?

Throughout this book, I will explain what it means to be **'authentic'** in my view and how it affects you in so many ways when we do not live in an **'authentic'** manner true to ourselves. Examples of this are when we go against our gut feeling or do something that we do not want to do that causes feelings of guilt, shame, anger, resentment, etc. Examples would include:

- Pretending to like something or someone: We often pretend to like things or people to fit in with a certain group or avoid offending others, even if it goes against our true preferences or values.

- Suppressing emotions: We sometimes suppress our emotions or put on a brave face to avoid appearing weak or vulnerable, even if it goes against our true feelings and can be harmful to our mental health.

- Hiding aspects of ourselves: We may hide certain aspects of ourselves, such as our sexuality or political beliefs, out of fear of judgment or rejection from others.

- Living up to others' expectations: We may try to live up to others' expectations of us, whether it's our parents, partners, or peers, even if it goes against our true desires or goals.

- Settling for less: We sometimes settle for less than what we truly want in life, whether it's a job, relationship, or lifestyle, out of fear of failure or societal pressure to conform to certain standards.

There is a tonne of literature written about being our true and authentic selves, and there is a whole host of differing professions that would analyze and dissect *'authenticity,'* including GPs, life coaches, psychologists, psychiatrists, psychotherapists, motivational speakers, etc. Different professionals have coined their own versions of authenticity, but most are, in essence, the same idea:

- *"We're born with a need for attachment and a need for authenticity." Most people abandon their true selves (authenticity) to please others and keep the relationships (attachments) even if they are ones that are toxic and destructive." – Gabor Mate*

- *"Authenticity is a collection of choices that we have to make every day."……. "If you trade your authenticity for safety, you may experience the following: anxiety, depression, eating disorders, addiction, rage, blame, resentment, and inexplicable grief." – Brene Brown*

- *"Most of your desires are not really about yourself. You just picked them up from your social surroundings." – Sadghuru*

- *"Everyone sees what you appear to be, few experience what you really are." - Niccolò Machiavelli*

Growing up in the Western world and, more acutely, the west of Scotland, I would imagine that most people would believe the word authenticity to mean *'to be real to themselves'* or *'to be honest,*

5

straight talking and to conform to social norms and state laws that have been made by other people.' This is not what I mean when talking of *'authenticity'*; I believe when someone is truly authentic to themselves, they are in full control of emotions, feelings, behaviors, etc., and are happy with the decisions they make and are truly happy with the life they have. Authenticity, I believe, is also intrinsically linked to 'awareness'. The *'authenticity'* I speak of is a rare commodity and rarely seen in our Westernised culture.

"With awareness comes choice. And so you are able to say "I allow this moment to be as it is". And then, suddenly before where there was irritation, there is now a sense of aliveness and peace. And out of that comes right action". – Eckhart Tolle

Having a level of 'awareness' allows us to challenge our own thoughts and behaviors and become aware of our emotions, feelings, behaviors, etc. This allows us to constantly check in on ourselves and act in a way that makes us happy and content with our choices; ultimately, you must become aware of both external and internal factors that disconnect you from yourself and cause a loss of attachment issues, which keeps us from being genuine. So, a certain level of awareness is needed to be *'authentic,'* and these levels of awareness differentiate in each individual.

"In our personal lives, if we do not develop our own self-awareness and become responsible for first creations, we empower other people and circumstances to shape our lives by default."
– Stephen Covey

"It is better to conquer yourself than to win a thousand battles."
– Gautama Buddha

"We must each lead a way of life with self-awareness and compassion, to do as much as we can. Then, whatever happens, we will have no regrets."
– Dalai Lama

Most of us go through life with a poor level of awareness as this is not something that we are taught from a young age. Going through life on autopilot allows us to conform to societal rules and gives most of us a sense of freedom. This could be argued to be false freedom, as most of us are bound by a rigid structure we have created in our minds that allows us to be the best versions of ourselves in this unauthentic society; unfortunately, this detached us from our true selves and identity and caused a conflict within, some worse than others. This is why I believe society has such shocking statistics on addiction, mental health problems, suicide, and crime rates, and these statistics lean towards showing that for most of society, we are unknowingly and subconsciously not being authentic to ourselves.

"I could never trust anyone who is well adjusted to a sick society."

– Andrea Gibson

"It's no measure of health to be well adjusted to a profoundly sick society."

- Jiddu Krishnamurti

"No society can understand itself without looking at its shadow self."

Authenticity in chaos
– Gabor Mate

This book will look at how I managed to survive in the prison environment at a great cost to my own authenticity. I will look at the lives of many of the individuals I encountered throughout my time in prison and explore the many different factors that cause them to be untrue to themselves, causing damage that, for the vast majority, cannot be fixed. I know many people have their views on prisoners, and I am not suggesting for one minute that I am right and they are wrong or trying to justify the acts of individuals; I am simply looking at an environment and giving my true evaluation of it. An environment that promotes a logo of **'transforming lives for the better'**. I struggle to accept or even empathize with this promotion. As life behind bars is transforming lives, 'but not for the better'. In my opinion, the vast majority transform for the worse, and hopefully, I can highlight this throughout the book.

I can only tell my truth and use my unique perspective to try and show the great tragedy happening within the extremely demanding, controlling, and authoritarian prison environment we have set up for people who do not adhere to state laws that society has legislated. I will not only look at the effects of unauthenticity on prisoners but will look at how it affects staff and how they are conditioned and forced to be an unauthentic version of themselves. I hope this book is insightful for people and can offer a different view and maybe even touch on some of the reasons why people cannot be the genuine article themselves.

Introduction:

This book takes you into the gritty reality of prison life, exploring the struggle to stay true to oneself in an environment that often feels like a separate society. Drawing from my own experiences serving a life sentence, I'll share stories of diverse characters, providing a broad perspective on the concept of authenticity in this challenging terrain.

Throughout these pages, we'll delve into the factors that hinder authenticity in prison. The rigid rules and punitive values clash with the human nature of connection, forcing individuals to adopt survival techniques that erode their genuine humanity. Prisoners must navigate a world that demands a version of themselves designed to endure the unnatural and inauthentic prison setting they've been thrust into.

In our journey, we'll witness the impact of learned behaviors that conflict with the 'authentic self,' leading to a range of mental health struggles. The harsh reality is that many prisoners, in their quest for survival, embark on a tumultuous journey away from their true selves, facing self-sabotage and identity crises. The pursuit of authenticity becomes a luxury, often lost in the chaotic confines of incarceration.

Authenticity, the quality of being true to oneself, is a fundamental need, as highlighted by experts in the field:

Dr. Gabor Mate emphasizes the link between authenticity and mental well-being.

Authenticity in chaos
Dr. Nicole LePera underscores the importance of self-awareness for authentic relationships.

Friedrich Nietzsche frames the journey to authenticity as the task of shaping oneself.

Carl Jung regards the privilege of a lifetime as becoming one's true self.

In the distorted reality of prison life, individuals are forced to don different masks, adapting to various situations or facing severe consequences. Many become institutionalized, struggling to rediscover their pre-prison selves. This journey, often marked by self-sacrifice and compromised identities, raises fundamental questions about the possibility of authenticity in a system that prioritizes control over personal well-being.

As we explore the microcosm of prison, we'll address critical questions:

How feasible is it to reclaim one's authentic self outside the survival mode?

Can we inadvertently construct mental prisons to find comfort in uncomfortable surroundings?

Do we build emotional walls to shield ourselves from the harsh reality?

What mental health challenges arise from disconnecting from our true selves?

This exploration shines a light on issues overlooked by authorities attempting to manage crime and incarceration. Some individuals find their true selves in prison, prompting reflection on the health of society beyond the prison walls. In the struggle to compromise core values for survival, we'll examine how both staff and prisoners are conditioned to sacrifice authenticity. It's an examination of how insanity can prevail in a chaotic world, echoing Einstein's words about doing the same thing repeatedly and expecting different results.

"Welcome to the exploration of authenticity in the midst of chaos."

Chapter One: What is a prison, and what is its ultimate purpose?

To explore the possibility of authenticity in a prison setting, we must first examine the purpose and realities of prison life. Different countries have varying views on prisons, with some being more liberal and others more punitive. In this book, we'll focus primarily on the Scottish Prison System (SPS), since I personally spent 15 years in that system. Although the public may have a certain perception of the SPS, my experience was vastly different. Nonetheless, it's important to approach the topic objectively and with as unbiased a perspective as possible. To provide context, below is the SPS's vision statement and values:

OUR VISION — Helping to build a safer Scotland, unlocking potential, transforming lives.

OUR MISSION — Providing services that help to transform the lives of people in our care so they can fulfil their potential and become responsible citizens.

OUR VALUES

BELIEF
We believe that people can change.

RESPECT
We have proper regard for individuals, their needs and their human rights.

INTEGRITY
We apply high ethical, moral and professional standa

OPENNESS
We work with others to achieve the best outcomes.

COURAGE
We have the courage to care regardless of circumstances.

HUMILITY
We cannot do this c our own, we recogr we can learn from o

We'll examine each of the SPS's mission statements and explore how they relate to the concept of authenticity and whether they facilitate or hinder one's connection to one's true self. It's worth noting that large institutions, particularly government ones like the SPS, often present a positive image in their mission statements, but the reality can be quite different. Throughout this book, I'll aim to support any personal statements or opinions I express with evidence and statistics.

"Helping to build a safer Scotland, unlocking potential and transforming lives."

Let's begin by examining the SPS's vision statement: "Helping to build a safer Scotland, unlocking potential and transforming lives." Essentially, the prison system aims to unlock individuals' authenticity and potential to transform their lives for the sake of a safer Scotland. While this sounds promising, the reality is often quite different from the image portrayed. In my experience, it's nearly impossible for prisoners to undergo such a transformation and become exemplary members of society. In fact, it's widely accepted that prisons are:

- *Violent*
- *Aggressive*
- *Drug fuelled*
- *Frightening*
- *Full of criminally minded people*
- *Us against them mentality*
- *Punitive*
- *Alien*
- *Unnatural*

Authenticity in chaos

Most of us have seen a TV series or movie about prison, but what's depicted on screen doesn't always capture the true reality of life behind bars. In fact, the reality can be much worse than what's portrayed on our screens. There are also popular podcasts featuring ex-prisoners discussing their experiences, but some of these individuals may be dramatizing or glorifying their time in prison to gain validation from the audience. This tendency to be unauthentic is a by-product of the prison environment, where vulnerability is often seen as weakness. Instead of sharing their true experiences and beginning to heal from the trauma of their time behind bars, some ex-prisoners feel compelled to present a false image to the world.

It's important to acknowledge the harsh realities of prison life and the impact it can have on individuals. The question then becomes, how can someone find their true self within this environment? It's worth noting that people are incarcerated for crimes against society, and in theory, the aim is to make Scotland a safer place. However, the flip side is that the prison environment can be dangerous and toxic, further alienating individuals from their true selves as they are forced to adopt a "survival of the fittest" mentality.

For those who have been victims of crime, it's understandable to want perpetrators to be held accountable for their actions. However, it's also important to recognize that the prison system itself can have negative effects on individuals' mental health and well-being, making it even more challenging to find one's true self. It's crucial that we strive for a justice system that not only holds people accountable for their actions but also provides support and resources to help them heal and connect with their authentic selves in order to truly rehabilitate.

It's important to acknowledge that most skilled criminals are not incarcerated, and the prison system is primarily filled with individuals who are struggling with drug addiction, mental health issues, and traumatic experiences. These factors often stem from a lack of authenticity and a lack of positive influences in their lives. It's difficult to imagine that anyone would intentionally choose a life of mental health problems and drug addiction, yet many individuals find themselves in this situation due to a variety of circumstances.

It's crucial that we address the underlying issues that lead to criminal behavior, such as poverty, trauma, and lack of access to mental healthcare, rather than simply punishing individuals for their actions. By creating a society that values authenticity and connection, we can help individuals heal and prevent them from ending up in the criminal justice system in the first place. The connection between mental health and addiction is defined as **'dual diagnosis,'** a word that explains, in my opinion, the vast majority of prisoners but is not a term widely used in a prison setting. The NHS defines it as,

"A severe mental illness combined with misuse of substances. Severe mental illness in this guideline includes a clinical diagnosis of: schizophrenia, schizotypal and delusional disorders, bipolar, affective disorder severe depressive episode(s) with or without psychotic episodes."

While the definition of dual diagnosis is helpful, I believe it's important to recognize that any mental health issue, regardless of severity, can have a significant impact on individuals, particularly in a prison setting where even minor issues can be magnified and lead to more significant problems. Mental health issues such as anxiety, depression, low mood, low self-esteem, and lack of confidence can

Authenticity in chaos

all be extremely challenging to manage, especially in the high-stress environment of prison.

According to findings.org.uk, it's crucial that we address mental health issues in the prison system, as they can lead to more significant problems such as addiction and exacerbate existing issues. By recognizing and addressing mental health issues, we can help individuals find the support and resources they need to manage their conditions and ultimately improve their overall well-being.

"Dual diagnosis is a common problem in prisons. "Nine out of ten people in prison have a mental health or substance abuse problem – often together – but most do not receive the right care." Many prisons in the UK apply a "parallel approach" to dual diagnosis, where patient care is provided by more than one treatment service at the same time." – findings.org.uk

I understand that many people may not be sympathetic towards prisoners or their struggles, but it's important to recognize the impact that the prison system can have on individuals. Despite the prisons' assertion that they are "helping to build a safer Scotland, unlocking potential, and transforming lives," I believe that their actions and policies often fall short of these goals.

While it's true that prisoners have committed crimes against society, it's also important to recognize that the prison system often fails to provide opportunities for individuals to connect with their authentic selves and make positive changes. This can lead to individuals becoming even more alienated and disconnected from society, which may ultimately result in them committing further crimes and perpetuating the cycle of incarceration. This can be backed up by the re-offending rates in Scotland:

- 2017-18: 26.3%

- 2018-19: 25.9%
- 2019-20: 24.8%
- 2020-21: 23.8%

While the reconviction rates in Scotland have been decreasing over the past decade, there is still a significant proportion of offenders who re-offend within the first year of their release from custody. This statistic raises serious concerns about the effectiveness of the current system in transforming lives and reducing re-offending rates.

In my opinion, this high re-offending rate is due to the lack of opportunities for individuals to connect with their authentic selves and make positive changes. The prison environment can be highly dehumanizing and can strip individuals of their identity and sense of self-worth. When they are released back into society, they may struggle to reintegrate and find meaning and purpose in their lives, leading to a higher risk of re-offending. Moreover, the reconviction rates for those who are convicted after the one-year threshold are extremely hard to obtain, suggesting that the current system may not be effectively addressing the root causes of criminal behavior or may be playing with statistics to make their system look better than it really is.

It's crucial that we work towards a justice system that prioritizes rehabilitation and personal growth and recognizes the importance of authenticity in the process of transformation. By providing individuals with the support and resources they need to connect with their authentic selves, we can help reduce re-offending rates and create a safer and more just society.
I believe that we must work towards a justice system that not only holds individuals accountable for their actions but also recognizes their humanity and provides opportunities for rehabilitation and

personal growth. By doing so, we can create a society that values and supports all individuals, regardless of their past mistakes or struggles.

To truly transform an individual's life, it's crucial to first understand their life, empathize with their struggles, and then guide them through a step-by-step, slow process of change and reintegration. This not only involves helping them navigate the **'unauthentic environment'** around them but also reconnecting them with themselves, a process that can be daunting and uncomfortable. Unfortunately, I believe that the Scottish Prison Service (SPS) does not have a budget that adequately covers such a complex transformation.

While the SPS may temporarily make Scotland safer by taking troubled individuals off the streets, there is no guarantee of real, lasting transformation within the prison system unless the prisoner is truly ready and committed to change. In my experience, the only way I have seen this change is often through a spiritual or theological awakening, in which the individual turns their back on the life that has failed them and embraces a new way of being. This being their choice to transform their life and not the prison's claim of transforming lives, I strongly disagree that there is much attempt by the system to transform people into their *'authentic'* selves.

Providing services to help transform the lives of people in our care so they can fulfil their potential and become responsible citizens

While the prison system in Scotland provides opportunities for prisoners to access various services to help them become responsible citizens, the reality is that few prisoners take advantage of these services. As a volunteer with third-sector organizations like

Sisco and Phoenix Futures, I witnessed firsthand the tremendous effort put into rebuilding the lives of lost prisoners, but unfortunately, the success rate is low in comparison to the number of prisoners who enter the system.

During my time in top-end conditions at HMP Barlinnie, I was part of a team that came up with a new concept of having a recovery café within the prison environment. This was a completely foreign idea to both staff and prisoners, and we faced numerous barriers in breaking down the obstacles regarding confidentiality, security, building trust and offering a service that was in high demand to only a few inmates. These challenges were only the beginning of the iceberg when attempting to establish such a radical concept in a security-driven environment. I and other team members, including Natalie Logan (Creator of Sisco) and Robert Kerr (HMP Barlinnie prison officer), worked tirelessly to convince the hierarchy of HMP Barlinnie that having a staff-free space was crucial if any healing was to occur within the recovery café. However, this was not an easy feat as there were many difficult situations to overcome, including the fact that prisoners had to get open and vulnerable about drug use, struggles of prison life, and their family issues, all while being in a constant, hyper-vigilant state.

It took many meetings and a lot of hard work to convince the prison system that a staff-free space was necessary to build trust and for prisoners to become vulnerable in such a hostile environment. But due to the dedication of everyone involved in the café and the tireless efforts of Natalie and Danny, one of the instrumental workers in convincing the system, the recovery café model was eventually rolled out to most, if not all, of the prisons in Scotland. The undertaking was a huge success and allowed prisoners to get vulnerable and truthful about aspects of their lives that were not their authentic selves, even their fake authentic selves from the conditioned society. Despite the challenges faced, the recovery café proved to be a useful tool for helping prisoners heal and transform their lives, and its success serves as a testament to the power of perseverance and hard work.

The concept of the recovery café provides a poignant example of the difficulties in introducing anything new into the prison system. The prison's primary concern is understandably security, and any novel ideas can often be perceived as a threat by the security team and the more punitive members of the hierarchy. It can sometimes feel like staff, with a more punitive approach take new ideas personally, such as the concept of the recovery café. This underscores the closed nature of the system when it comes to embracing new ideas that prioritize authenticity and rehabilitation.

The system's reluctance to change can be frustrating, especially for those working to bring positive change to the prison environment. However, it's important to recognize that change takes time and that it often requires a concerted effort from multiple stakeholders. While new concepts may face resistance, it's essential to continue advocating for meaningful reform that prioritizes rehabilitation and the well-being of prisoners.

Despite the presence of third-sector groups within the prison system, I have personally witnessed organizations sending people into the prison environment, particularly recovery agencies, with zero attendance. This not only highlights the lack of desire for change among most prisoners but also the deep-seated mistrust between prisoners and any agency permitted to operate within the prison walls. This mistrust makes it challenging for any new organization to enter such a hostile environment and deliver a truly empathetic and soul-searching service. The "us against them" mentality that prevails within prisons, exacerbates the problem. While it may be somewhat better than it used to be, there is still conditioning on both sides that prevents staff and cons from trusting, engaging with, respecting, and empathizing with one another.

The lack of healing taking place on both sides only further cements the mistrust that keeps a significant barrier between staff and prisoners. This is a significant problem that must be addressed if any progress is to be made in transforming the prison system. It's crucial to recognize the profound impact of this mistrust and to work towards fostering greater trust and empathy between staff and prisoners. Only then can meaningful change occur. *'The Stanford Prison Experiment'* is a great example of how prisoners and staff mistrust each other:

The Stanford Prison Experiment was a landmark study conducted in 1971 by psychologist Philip Zimbardo at Stanford University. The study aimed to investigate how social and situational factors influence human behavior, particularly within the context of power dynamics and authority.

The study recruited 24 male participants who were randomly assigned to the role of either a prisoner or a guard in a simulated prison environment. The participants were screened for psychological and medical conditions and were told to act out their respective roles as realistically as possible.

The experiment was intended to last for two weeks, but it was terminated after just six days due to the extreme and disturbing behavior that emerged from both the guards and the prisoners. The guards became increasingly authoritarian and abusive, while the

Authenticity in chaos

prisoners became passive and submissive, with some developing psychological symptoms such as anxiety, depression, and even psychosis.

The study illustrated the profound impact of power dynamics and authority on human behavior, particularly in closed and controlled environments such as prisons. It also highlighted the lack of trust that can exist between different groups, in this case, between the guards and the prisoners.

The guards saw themselves as having complete control and dominance over the prisoners, while the prisoners felt powerless and oppressed. This power imbalance led to a breakdown in communication and empathy, with both groups becoming increasingly entrenched in their respective roles and identities.

Overall, the Stanford Prison Experiment underscores the importance of building trust and fostering open communication between different groups, particularly within high-pressure and controlled environments such as prisons. It also emphasizes the need to recognize the impact of power dynamics and authority on human behavior and to work towards creating more egalitarian and humane systems. The Stanford Experiment is a good way to describe the nature of the playing field in a prison setting, and in my opinion, the essential mistrust that incorporates the experiment is still well and truly alive in the prison system.

When asked if they trust what a prisoner tells them, most staff members would answer truthfully that they do not. Conversely, if a prisoner were asked if they believe what the staff tells them, the answer would likely be a general "no." This lack of trust from the very beginning undermines the prison system's stated commitment to providing services that help transform lives and promote responsible citizenship.

As someone who has spent 15 years in the system, I can attest to the fact that there is a small minority of staff who genuinely care about the well-being of prisoners and work to build their character and promote responsible citizenship. However, in my experience, the vast majority are not interested or trained enough to provide adequate care and support for prisoners' mental health and struggles within the prison. While there have been moments when staff have surprised me with acts of kindness or humility, most of the time, they are conditioned to devalue and detach prisoners from their authenticity. This conditioning further undermines the already fragile trust between staff and prisoners and perpetuates a culture of degradation and detachment that makes it difficult for prisoners to receive the care and support they need.

It is absolutely crucial to recognize the immense challenge of being responsible in a prison setting. The impact of conditioning on staff cannot be ignored, and it is essential to work towards creating a culture of trust and empathy within the prison system. Without this, any meaningful change will be impossible. The prisoners desperately need support to transform their lives and become responsible citizens, but the question must be asked: how can they learn the meaning of responsibility when the prison system effectively strips them of all aspects of it? This is a deeply difficult and complex issue that requires an empathetic and compassionate approach, which, unfortunately, is hard to balance out in a prison environment.

Our Values: Belief, Respect, Integrity, Openness, Courage, Humility

Authenticity in chaos

The relationship between the prison and its staff is absolutely critical, but unfortunately, it is not always what it seems. The prison system promotes values such as belief, respect, integrity, openness, courage, and humility, giving the impression of hope and rehabilitation. While some staff may genuinely embody these values, and some courses like the violence course, cog skills, and substance abuse courses explore them, the reality is far more complex. The truth is that prisoners know what staff want from them, and there is often a sense of dishonesty between the two parties. This leads to a pointless system where both prisoners and staff are aware that they are lying to each other, resulting in a tick-box approach where prisoners say what staff want to hear to progress through the system. The relationship between the prison and its staff is essential, but it must be based on honesty, trust, and a genuine desire to help prisoners transform their lives.

'Belief': The value of "belief" in people's ability to change, as seen in the Scottish Prison System's manifesto, is a misguided and outdated notion. It is concerning that they feel the need to state it as a value, which suggests that they are far behind in creating a system that truly allows people to heal and transform. The truth is that there is ample evidence that people can change with the right support and help, not just in Scotland but around the world. Highlighting "belief" as a value is simply an attempt to give the impression of faith in the prisoners, which is meaningless without real action and tangible support.

Furthermore, "belief" should not even be a value in question; it is self-evident that people can change. Everyone knows someone in their life who has overcome addiction or used personal growth tools to become the best version of themselves. Therefore, the focus should be on providing prisoners with the necessary tools, resources, and opportunities to transform their lives and become responsible citizens. People can change, and it is a fact, not a value that needs to be paraded on a manifesto by such an important institution as the Scottish Prison System. This argument shows that change is deeply needed in the system, and hopefully, the system can take action to create a more supportive and transformative environment.

'Respect': The word "respect" is a critical concept in prison, but it appears that the Scottish Prison System (SPS) may be misguided on how it uses this term in its values. The SPS claims to have proper regard for individuals and their human rights, suggesting that prisoners are living with respect from staff and given the best opportunity to change positively. However, in the next chapter of my book, I will delve into the real prison environment and highlight how the word "respect" takes on a whole different meaning. The truth of the matter is that there is very little respect between staff and prisoners, and this is not hard to believe.

In a prison setting, gaining mutual respect between staff and prisoners is an incredibly challenging task. As Tony Robbins aptly states, *"What makes a relationship work is things in common, what makes it passionate is that things are very different."* However, in a prison setting, prisoners and staff have vastly different mindsets and are taught opposing survival skills. For example, prisoners are often taught to mistrust authority figures and may view staff members as their oppressors. Conversely, staff members may view prisoners as dangerous and untrustworthy, making it challenging to develop mutual respect. This lack of mutual respect can have significant implications for the well-being of prisoners and staff alike. Research has shown that creating a culture of mutual respect and understanding can have a significant impact on reducing violence and increasing positive outcomes in prison settings. However, achieving this goal is far easier said than done. The Scottish Prison System (SPS) is particularly challenged in this regard, as it is far from the reality of the situation. Without a commitment to creating a culture of mutual respect and understanding, prisoners and staff will continue to be at odds, making it difficult to create a healing and transformative environment. While it is a daunting task, it is crucial to work towards bridging the gap between prisoners and staff to create a safer, more supportive prison system for all involved.

The concept of respect is touted as a core value within the SPS, yet the reality is far from what is projected. The vast majority of staff do not respect prisoners, and likewise, prisoners do not respect staff. This lack of proper regard for respect is a pervasive issue in the prison system, making it nearly impossible for anyone to be their authentic self. In such an environment, individuals are forced to battle with being disrespected and acting in a manner that is not respectful, which is not congruent with their authentic selves. This lack of authenticity can make healing difficult, as individuals are constantly undermined and forced to play a character that is not true to themselves.

This is a crucial issue that will be explored in detail in the next chapter of my book. If we are to create a system that truly allows individuals to heal and transform, we must address this fundamental lack of respect and work towards fostering an environment of mutual understanding and genuine respect for all. Thus, claiming respect as a core value within the SPS is misleading at best, in my opinion. Throughout the book, I will show how this claim is misguided and will provide reasons and examples of this on many occasions. While respect is an essential concept in prison, it is crucial to acknowledge that it is for all the wrong reasons, not for the reasons that the prison system would like to claim.

'Integrity': The prison system claims to uphold high, ethical, moral, and professional standards, but this claim may only be evident when presenting the system to the legislative or executive branches of the political system; certainly not evident on the front line in the halls of the prisons. The reality is far from the idealistic image projected by the system. As I delve into this book, I will show the application of high ethical and moral standards in a prison system characterized by trauma, mental health problems, addiction, poverty and violence is an incredibly challenging task, and the truth is the prison system is working within a tight budget is severely understaffed and has high expectations placed on it.

The prison system's failure to consistently apply high ethical, moral, and professional standards is not just a problem for those within the system; it has far-reaching implications for society as a whole. The fake authenticity perpetuated by the system has a corrosive effect on our collective values and beliefs. It would be more authentic and true if the prison system were to recognize these problems and not highlight them as one of their values. Nicola Machiavelli says, *"Whoever desires to found a state and give it laws must start with assuming that all men are bad and ever ready to display their vicious nature, whenever they may find occasion for it."* The system, unfortunately, would be better off claiming Nicola's words as their values rather than suggesting a level of high integrity and professionalism.

Throughout this book, I will provide many examples of how this value is severely compromised on many levels. These stories and experiences will both shock and prove that these core values are a self-invented myth that no one who truly knows the system actually believes. When an institution claims values that they know themselves are questionable at best, it creates a counter-productive environment that undermines the very goals it seeks to achieve. The moral and professional standards that are in place within the system can even hinder authenticity. If we are to create a prison system that genuinely allows individuals to heal and become their authentic selves, we must acknowledge this fundamental issue. The fake authenticity perpetuated by the system has a damaging impact on society as a whole, and it is time to address it and work towards creating a system that is truly authentic and values-driven.

'Openness': It's important to highlight the illogical nature of promoting openness between staff and prisoners within a prison environment. Openness is a wonderful concept, and the fact that there is a rare person to whom a prisoner or staff member can be open is priceless. However, the harsh reality of the situation is that being open whilst in prison is both counter-productive for progressing through the system and dangerous within the predatory hall environment. These are the stark realities of prison life, and trying to sugarcoat it with misleading manifestos makes no real change or gives no hope for the healing process to begin; authenticity requires openness, and this is a concept, in reality, both staff and prisoner (if being truthful) would advise against in most situations in prison.

Although some staff members may be trustworthy, and prisoners may confide in someone they trust, the truth is that openness within a prison environment can be unwise and even dangerous due to the prevalence of violence and underlying tensions.

It's important to keep in mind that the majority of time is spent within the confines of the prison walls, where prisoners must utilize tools and methods that are best suited for survival in that harsh environment. Unfortunately, the concept of **"openness"** - which is often equated with authenticity - can be a liability in the violent and drug-fueled halls of a prison. Thus, it's only logical for individuals within the prison system to maintain a sense of closure, which is the opposite of openness. As much as we might value transparency and honesty in other areas of life, the reality of the prison environment necessitates a different approach to interpersonal communication and trust-building. Although some level of openness may exist between staff members and other professionals within the prison system, the way in which the concept of openness is portrayed in the manifesto is misleading. It suggests that there is a level of trust and openness between everyone in the prison, which is simply not the case. Throughout the book, I will provide examples that demonstrate the impracticality of promoting openness within the prison environment, especially between staff and prisoners. While there may be a few individuals who can be trusted, the harsh reality of the prison system makes true openness a risky and potentially dangerous proposition.

'Courage': Courage is a vital attribute for survival in prison, and for prisoners, being true to oneself is one of the most courageous acts that can be undertaken. This applies equally to staff members, particularly those who work on the front line in the halls and who must also contend with the pressure to conform to prison norms. However, the notion that "we have the courage to care regardless of circumstances" - as touted in the manifesto - is nothing more than propaganda. In reality, the only courage that can be found in a prison setting is when an individual tries to break free from the toxic mold of prison societal norms and become their authentic self. This is a rare occurrence and usually happens when a prisoner turns to a theological path. Throughout the book, I will highlight examples of courage within the prison system and the challenges that come with

Authenticity in chaos

embracing authenticity. Despite the opposition to authenticity that exists within prison norms, there is a voice for courage that deserves to be heard.

'Humility': The most truthful aspect of the prison manifesto may be the recognition that "we cannot do this on our own, we recognize we can learn from others." Very few staff and prisoners would argue that the prison system needs radical change if there is any hope of becoming a more authentic version of itself. Unfortunately, the current system is an unauthentic version of rehabilitation. It's encouraging to see recognition of the need for change and the willingness to listen to others, but this is rarely put into practice. It is precisely this lack of humility and failure to implement necessary changes that have led the prison system to its current state. Throughout the book, we will explore in detail and examine statistics on modern-day prisons to illustrate just how much humility is needed within the system. Authenticity is the change that is required, and it's time for the prison system to embrace it.

Chapter Two: Confronting Incarceration: The Genesis of My Prison Story

Life within prison walls is undoubtedly a difficult experience, and this is something that society and the media often sensationalize. In Scotland, the justice system is built around a punitive approach aimed at punishing those who have committed crimes against society. Consequently, the prison population is incredibly diverse, made up of individuals who have committed a broad range of offenses, ranging from minor incidents like shoplifting to much more serious crimes such as murder.

Regardless of the specific crimes committed, all prisoners are placed under the care of the state and confined within the same walls. This can create an incredibly challenging and often volatile environment, which can make the experience of serving a sentence all the more daunting for those who find themselves incarcerated. Throughout the book, we will explore the complexities and realities of prison life, shining a light on the experiences of those who are all too often overlooked or stigmatized by society. By exploring the unique challenges and experiences of prisoners, we can foster greater understanding and empathy, challenging the harmful narratives perpetuated by the media and society at large.

It's worth noting that the media often portrays prison life in a particular way, with a focus on the more sensational or negative aspects, and can downplay the harsh realities and extremely wavy navigation that individuals face in prison. This can perpetuate misconceptions and stereotypes about what life is truly like within the prison system and can be damaging for those who have already been punished by society for their crimes. Headlines like:

- **Exclusive: Convicts riot in luxury Addiewell Prison eight weeks after it opens – Daily Record**

- **IN THE NICK OF TIME Tough Scots prison ranked as second cushiest in the WORLD for cons – The Sun**

- **Britain's LUXURY prisons: Inside the jails where lags live like kings – Daily Star**

These sensational headlines are painting a false picture of prison life, where they suggest that inmates live like royalty. But let me assure you, this couldn't be further from the truth. While there may be some prisoners who appear to be living better than others, this is not a reflection of the reality of life in prison. The notion of a "holiday camp" is completely untrue and perpetuated by the media for their own gain. Living like a king in a prison setting may seem appealing to some, but it's important to recognize the inherent fruitlessness of such a lifestyle. Being a king among prisoners only means you're the leader of a group of individuals who are considered at the bottom of society. In other words, it's a meaningless title that carries no real significance.

Furthermore, living like a king in prison does not equate to a peaceful and content life. It's an unauthentic way of living, and while it may seem like an easy life to some, the reality is quite the opposite. The truth is that being a king in prison is ultimately worthless and a poor substitute for true freedom and a fulfilling life.

The journey to prison can be a complex and overwhelming experience for those who find themselves in the criminal justice system. It often involves a lengthy process of court appearances, legal proceedings, and assessments before a decision is ultimately made to impose a custodial sentence. Throughout this book, we will delve into the intricacies of the prison system and the experiences of those who are confined within its walls.

By shedding light on the realities of prison life and addressing common misconceptions, we can cultivate greater understanding and empathy for those who are often forgotten or demonized by society. As a poignant reminder of the harsh reality of prison life, I'd like to share a powerful poem written by a judge in the USA.

The poem beautifully captures the essence of life behind bars and reminds us of the human cost of imprisonment:

We want them to have self-worth - So we destroy their self-worth

We want them to be responsible - So we take away all responsibility

We want them to be positive and constructive - So we degrade them and make them useless

We want them to be trustworthy - So we put them where there is no trust.

We want them to quit exploiting us - So we put them where they exploit each other.

We want them to take control of their lives and quit being a parasite on us - So we make them totally dependent on us.

Authenticity in chaos

We want them to quit hanging around losers - So we put all the losers in the state under one roof.

We want them to quit being the tough guy - So we put them where the tough guy is respected.

We want them to be non-violent - So we put them where violence is all around them.

We want them to be kind and loving people - So we subject them to hatred and cruelty

-Judge Dennis A. Challeen

It's fascinating to see a judge acknowledging the need for change within the system through the medium of poetry. Judge Challeen's poem provides a powerful insight into the realities of prison life, highlighting the stark contrast between the notion of authenticity and the truth of confinement. As someone who has personally experienced life behind bars, I can attest to the accuracy of Judge Challeen's observations. His words cut to the heart of the matter and capture the essence of what it means to be locked up. Moving on to my time in prison, I can say that it was a challenging experience that forced me to confront my own shortcomings and re-evaluate my priorities, stealing my identity and 'authenticity' in the process.

It's important to note that this book is not about my case or wrongful conviction. However, I can say that my time in prison was an incredibly challenging experience from the very beginning. In 2005, I was wrongfully convicted of murder and found myself navigating the complexities of the criminal justice system.

Rather, it delves into the broader issues surrounding prison life and the struggle to maintain one's sense of self in a chaotic and often unforgiving environment. For those who have never experienced life behind bars, it can be difficult to imagine the sheer magnitude of the challenges faced by those who are incarcerated.

As I recount my experiences, I hope to shed light on the realities of prison life and the toll it takes on one's sense of identity and authenticity. While my case may have been unique, the issues I explore in this book are universal and affect countless individuals who have found themselves caught up in the criminal justice system.

When I was convicted and sent to prison at just 20 years old, I was transported to HMYOI Polmont - a young offender's institute. While there may have been changes since my time there, I can only speak to my own experiences within these walls. One of the biggest challenges of the journey to prison was the feeling of being dehumanized and stripped of all personal belongings. As someone who has just been found guilty of a serious crime, I understand that many people believe that harsh treatment of criminals is justified. But it's important to remember that those who are incarcerated are still human beings, deserving of basic dignity and respect.

The experience of being transported in the 'reliance' (now GEOamey) van was the start of an incredibly traumatic experience for me. As I left behind my "normal" life, I was acutely aware that I was entering into an entirely foreign and frightening experience - the world of prison. But this was only the beginning of a journey that would prove to be one of the most challenging and transformative experiences of my life. Imprisonment challenged my sense of identity and authenticity in ways that I could never have imagined.

While some may argue that criminals deserve to suffer in prison, it's important to recognize the human cost of such a mentality. The experience of imprisonment is a deeply personal one, with the potential to strip individuals of their sense of self and leave them struggling to reclaim their identity. It's crucial to approach these issues with empathy and an open mind, recognizing the complexities of the criminal justice system and its profound impact on those who find themselves caught up in it. Only by doing so can we begin to address the challenges of prison life and work towards a more just and humane system that nurtures some sort of *'authenticity.'*

Arriving in Polmont prison, you are immediately stripped of your identity and reduced to a mere number: 87354. The entrance is a fearful sight, filled with the deafening sounds of other prisoners shouting and talking while they wait in tiny "dug boxes." And unbeknown then comes the strip search - a humiliating experience that leaves you completely vulnerable. You are forced to squat down naked, with some staff even demanding to inspect your foreskin. This is a humiliating experience that you learn to live with. Unfortunately, this part of life becomes normal behaviour as you are routinely and regularly inspected this way after visits or during cell searches. Normalization and desensitization are huge parts of the destruction of *'authenticity.'*

While you can understand the need for security measures, it's difficult to reconcile with the values claimed by the Scottish Prison Service (SPS) of humanity, dignity, and integrity. It would be more honest for the SPS to acknowledge that it's a punitive system operating on a tight budget, which does its best to signpost prisoners to third-sector organizations. As a young 20-year-old, you feel utterly powerless when faced with two full-grown men who have complete control over your body. Refusing to comply with their demands carries severe consequences, such as being forcefully thrown into "the digger" - a type of solitary confinement - until the staff are satisfied with the outcome. The indescribable fear and vulnerability that you experience in that moment is overwhelming.

After the strip search, I was sent to Spey Hall, also known as Ally Calley, in 2005. This hall was reserved for remand prisoners and was known to be a rough place. I stayed there for four weeks until I was taken to the High Court in Glasgow, where I was given a 15-year sentence with a life license. Facing both the victim's family and my own family was an overwhelming experience. I had to put on a facade and summon the courage to be strong for them, even though it felt like an impossible task. Lady Rita Rae accused me of deceiving the entire community into believing that I was a decent person despite receiving numerous positive character references before the sentencing procedure. It was an unwinnable situation, and I felt completely surreal.

Looking back on the whole situation, it still brings back uncomfortable feelings of anxiety, fear, and trauma. It can trigger a whole chain of reactions and emotions that consciously and subconsciously affect my mental health. As an accused, there is no support during this process, which may be understandable from the public's perspective, but the trauma that the high court procedure can bring is often overlooked. Is this the way things are, or can we do better? Does it matter that the accused has no support? These are all questions that will have differing views depending on who you ask. The fact remains that the court procedure can cause deep resentment and trauma for a lot of people, and most of the time, this is only the start of the trauma to come.

That night, I was told I'd be transferred to North Wing since I was now a convicted criminal. This was an old hall reserved for short-term prisoners, and it was my first time witnessing serious violence in the prison setting. Little did I know, it would not be the last. A boy was slashed with a razor while hanging over a pool table, and the sight was utterly horrifying. The staff scrambled to intervene as the deafening noise of a riot bell went off. But what struck me was the sheer normality of this horrific situation. People were laughing, desensitized to the violence within the prison walls.

The normalization of violence in prisons takes a toll on one's authentic self. Witnessing or experiencing violent altercations creates fear and forces individuals to build emotional walls to protect themselves. This hypervigilance affects both prisoners and staff, making it difficult to be true to oneself. It takes a significant toll on one's psyche. However, I don't want the book to focus solely on my time in prison. Let's summarize it briefly and move on to discussing how this normalization of violence affects our authenticity.

Chapter Three: Surviving the Storm: Examining the Impact of Prison Violence

When discussing the prison environment, it is absolutely crucial to address the devastating impact of violence on one's psyche. It is an ever-present and traumatic event that shatters the lives of those who are forced to endure it within these walls. Violence is something that is completely foreign to the majority of the population and is not encountered in their daily lives. However, within a prison environment, this is a complete reversal. Violence is not only commonplace but is often celebrated in ways that society outside of prison cannot comprehend.

The normalization of violence within the prison system can have a profound effect on the authenticity of the individuals within it, causing them to adopt a twisted and skewed perception of what is acceptable and normal behaviour in society. The more violent an individual is within the prison system, the more they are feared, and this can build a paradoxical sense of safety for them.

Violence comes in all shapes and forms within prisons, from a simple 'square go' to a brutal murder. The spectrum of violent acts in prison is wide and devastating. To survive in a prison setting, one must harden oneself against the possibility of violence and become self-sufficient in dealing with the prospect of violence at any moment. The fear of violence that prisoners and staff face on a daily basis forces them to build walls up, both consciously and subconsciously, to cope with the extreme fear that these violent acts and threats have on their psyche and body.

It cannot be stressed enough how violence in a prison setting fundamentally affects authenticity. The trauma and scars left by violence linger long after physical wounds have healed, leaving witnesses and victims alike struggling to find healing and growth. The harsh reality of violence in prison does not allow for personal authenticity or genuine self-discovery.

This truth is exemplified by the recent report into HMP Addiewell, revealing that 40 percent of inmates experienced abuse, threats, bullying, or assault by staff, with just 29 percent feeling safe most or all of the time. Such violence is not a new problem, as shown by the 2010 riots that left two guards injured at HMP Addiewell. However, despite reports and promises to rehabilitate and provide purposeful activity, the underlying current of underworld activity and pressure to manipulate statistics for the sake of company or personal agenda, fosters an environment of 'unauthenticity.' Walls are built to protect pain and suffering, turning prisoners and staff alike into distorted versions of themselves.

Authenticity in chaos

These trauma-building factories do not allow for healing or personal growth, which has consequences not only for the prisoner but for society as a whole. When these prisoners are released back into society, they can be 'loaded canons' *'or'* 'at the very least working on themselves'. The vicious cycle will continue until we recognize that the problem lies in the mistrust and the need to become unauthentic to survive. How can people find their true selves in such conditions? The answer is simple: they cannot. Violence in prison fundamentally undermines authenticity and healing, perpetuating a cycle of trauma and 'unauthenticity.'

Anyone can google the facts, and there is a huge amount of articles and academic papers written that show the huge amount of serious violence in Scottish prisons. Here are just a few of the newspaper articles:

April 2023:

"The report revealed that 40 percent of inmates had experienced abuse, threats, bullying, or assault by staff, while just 29 percent felt safe all or most of the time. The prison's poor access to healthcare, levels of cleanliness, and inadequate fresh air provisions were also highlighted as areas of concern. The chief inspector of prisons, Wendy Sinclair-Gieben, said that it was the worst treatment of inmates she had encountered during her term of office, and she will return for an unannounced visit to check progress before the next scheduled inspection in four years' time."

This story was from 2021:

A whistleblower from inside the <u>*HMP Addiewell*</u> *prison has described a working environment where prison custody officers live in fear as their superiors abandon them at every turn.*

Our source, who cannot be named out of fear of losing their job and, in turn, livelihood, claims that the last three weeks have seen a major security breach as well as a mass brawl that saw two prison officers taken to <u>hospital</u>.

<u>This story from 2010:</u>

HMP Addiewell: After riots leave two guards injured, critics warn of cash constraints in private prisons

IT WAS hailed as a jail of the future. But just a year after opening and rocked by a series of controversies, HMP Addiewell has only served to reignite the debate about whether prisons should be privately run at all.

<u>May 2023:</u>

Almost half of all inmates at a Scottish prison have told inspectors they had been abused, threatened, bullied, or assaulted by staff.

HM Inspectorate of Prisons for <u>Scotland</u> (HMIPS) visited HMP Addiewell in West Lothian in November last year and released a report on its findings on Thursday, raising significant concerns about the "enduring challenges" impacting the safety and security of the facility.

<u>September 2019:</u>

Over the same period, the prison population soared to one of the highest in Europe, up by 9% to 8,212, while costs increased. The European average for imprisonment is 117 per 100,000 population; in Scotland, it stands at 150 per 100,000 and is expected to increase further.

"Prisoner numbers exceed the operating capacity of Scotland's prisons and delays in upgrading the prison estate is increasing the

risk of failure," <u>her report said</u>. "SPS's performance is showing concerning trends, including growing prisoner violence and high and rising staff sickness absence."

The report highlighted:

Significant increases in assaults on staff by prisoners.

Stress-related illnesses among staff rose by nearly a third last year.

Financial pressures harm attempts to prepare and support prisoners for life outside prison.

January 2021:

Scots prisoner dies after throat slashed in brutal jail cell attack

These stories are in stark contrast to the perceived reality that the SPS and government would like to portray. An example is HMP Addiewell's internet homepage, where they write:

HMP Addiewell

At Sodexo Justice, we aim to change lives for the better by operating safe, decent, and secure prisons. We rehabilitate those in our care and provide purposeful activity, employment, education, and rehabilitation services. We support offenders to lead law-abiding lives in their community on release.

At HMP Addiewell, we run the full prison operations, including Prison Custody Officers and integrated Facilities Management, and we provide rehabilitation services, resettlement programs, *offender behavior programs, education and skills development, vocational training, and workshops and industries.*

We work in partnership with many different organizations and charities to improve the outcomes for the men in our care. Our partners share our vision and help us to achieve our aim to change lives for the better.

Our prison population demographic is complex and diverse, but our regime caters for everyone.

The prison inspectorate's report from April 2023 is the polar opposite of the reality inside the prison walls. In an inauthentic and statistic-driven world, the pressure to appear successful and meet certain benchmarks can cause companies, individuals, and even staff to manipulate the truth and statistics to suit their agenda. The truth is that prison is an incredibly dangerous place, with an underlying current of underworld activity that makes everyone in its toxic environment become an inauthentic version of themselves. Walls are built up to protect against the pain and suffering that exists within these trauma-building factories.

The false values that prisons place on themselves and present to the government, and the public are nothing but a façade. While some may argue that prisoners deserve their punishment, the fact remains that they will be released back into society one day. Would you rather have a loaded pistol or an unloaded one? The vicious cycle of violence in prison will continue until we acknowledge that the problem lies with mistrust and the pressure to become an inauthentic version of oneself to survive, both for prisoners and staff. It's impossible to achieve healing or true self-discovery in such an environment. Until we address the root causes of these issues,

Authenticity in chaos

the whole system will remain inauthentic, no matter how many analytical or statistical reports are done.

Returning to my experience in prison, the initial exposure to violence was deeply unsettling. However, it's remarkable how quickly the psyche adapts to this new environment, and violence becomes a common occurrence throughout one's time in prison. The longer you stay, the more violence you witness, and the further away your true, authentic self seems to drift; this is the reality for both staff and prisoners. What was once a horrific thing to see becomes normalized and even celebrated by the majority of prisoners, who are drawn to the alluring reputation of being violent. For some, this is a coping mechanism in a world where fear and demonization are prevalent. The more violent a person is, the less likely others are to confront them, making this an attractive prospect for many inmates who struggle daily with bullying, victimisation, and hypervigilance.

After being transferred to Iona Hall in Polmont, I felt relieved to find myself in a more modern building with better facilities. The absence of slopping out ((*Slopping out is a practice in prison where prisoners are required to use a bucket or chamber pot as a toilet during the night and then empty the contents of the bucket in the morning*) was particularly welcome, as it's a degrading and unpleasant experience that only adds to one's sense of worthlessness. Although the cells were more modern, the fact is that a cell is still a cell. In Iona Hall, I was placed in the long-term section, where I met a variety of individuals. One thing that struck me was the prevalence of inmates from impoverished backgrounds and working-class housing schemes. The class divide was immediately apparent, and it remained a constant throughout my time in prison. Over the course of 15 years, I only encountered a handful of people who weren't from working-class origins. For instance, it wasn't uncommon for there to be ten young people from Possilpark in Glasgow in the same hall at once - all friends of mine - many of whom have since passed away from murder, drugs, alcohol, or suicide.

I vividly recall listening to the narratives shared by these remarkable individuals aged between 16 and 21, and it struck me with immense gratitude for the loving family I had been fortunate enough to have. Their stories, however, were profoundly heartbreaking, as these young men had endured circumstances that were far from ordinary or conducive to healthy personal development. Astonishingly, they seemed unaware of the inherent wrongness in their upbringing, lacking the self-awareness to recognize the detrimental effects it had on their journey toward becoming their most authentic selves.

Living amidst an environment characterized by rebellion against authority and pervasive chaos had become the norm for these young men. Paradoxically, this familiarity with tumultuous and traumatic experiences granted them an unexpected advantage within the intricate web of the court system and the prison milieu in which we all found ourselves. Regrettably, the very adults employed in the prison ecosystem, from healthcare professionals to social workers, prison officers to governors, and even the individuals assigned to assist these young men with addiction and mental health concerns, had themselves been shaped by the traumatic and chaotic nature of the young men incarcerated in the young offenders.

Some of these young men would be in prison many, many times during my fifteen years of incarceration. This leads to the institutionalisation of many of the prison population. The timeframe for becoming institutionalised in prison can vary greatly from person to person. It depends on various factors, including the individual's background, length of incarceration, and the specific characteristics of the prison environment. However, there is no fixed or universally agreed-upon duration for the process of institutionalisation.

Authenticity in chaos

However, it is not hard to imagine that in a rigid structure in a toxic environment, where your mind needs to adapt to new morally and personally testing challenges, you lose part of yourself in the process.

Some individuals may experience a relatively quick adaptation to the prison environment, particularly if they have prior experience with the criminal justice system or if they are confronted with a highly regimented and restrictive prison setting. Others may take longer to adjust or may resist assimilating into the prison culture, but it is fair to say that whatever your background is, there can be no doubt about the way a person must change to adapt to the new environment. Institutionalisation is not an inevitable outcome for all prisoners. Factors such as strong social support, access to educational or rehabilitative programs, and individual resilience can mitigate the effects of institutionalisation and promote successful reintegration into society. These are the values promoted by the SPS, and this is what they aspire to offer prisoners, but with the current legislation and societal expectations of 'what a prison should be?', it is extremely hard to implement healing and beneficial apparatus that allow for prisoners to be 'authentic.'

I only spent seven months in HMYOI Polmont, so I was definitely not anywhere near institutionalised, but the violence and undercurrent of aggressive prison politics take their toll rapidly. I had to change my approach to people as a whole by adopting a more vigilant, assertive, and unkind way. At the start, I would help anyone by helping buy tea or coffee, tobacco, etc., but as time went on, other inmates and staff would point out that you were being used and often make fun of your kind nature until gradually you became less generous; traits like generosity and kindness can often be displayed as weakness in the prison environment, and it is not rare to hear inmates say things like, "that dafty is taking my saftness for daftness." Staff will warn you when you first arrive that you need to stick up for yourself and watch out for bullies and predators. Polmont very quickly teaches you a set of rules and values that you must adopt, and none of these, I can assure you, are what the SPS preach they value.

Chapter Four: Authenticity Under Siege: The Influence of HMP Shotts

Following my time at Polmont, I found myself, at the age of 21, heading to HMP Shotts—a maximum-security prison notorious for housing Scotland's most infamous inmates. Shotts was reserved for individuals serving long-term sentences, ranging from four years and beyond. Strangely enough, Shotts proved to be a breath of fresh air in comparison to Polmont, as it exhibited a comparatively calmer atmosphere with fewer outbursts of violence and aggression.

However, when contrasted with life outside the prison walls, the underlying current of prison politics remained unrelenting. Throughout my journey within the Scottish prison system, I encountered individuals who reveled in the chaotic nature of young offenders' institutions, missing the everyday violence and drama that pervaded that environment. It was a stark indication of how far removed these young men were from their true selves. Thriving in an environment replete with drugs, violence, and aggression meant there was no space for personal growth. The fact that some of us found solace in such circumstances highlights just how disconnected we had become from our authentic selves, some while incarcerated and others from their chaotic lives as a youngster.

What I seemed to notice in the adult prison was the huge change in the drug scene. Whilst Polmont had massive drug problems, Shotts had a drug culture like I had never seen before. I was in the NIC

Authenticity in chaos

(National Induction Centre). This hall was for people doing ten years and above, a kind of settling-in hall for a long-term sentence; the vast majority of prisoners in this hall were lifers. Every time someone was convicted of murder in the newspapers, they would arrive within a couple of weeks of being sentenced.

As human beings, part of our 'authentic' self is a free human, and this is why many philosophers and our great ancestors speak so highly of its value:

"Freedom is not just a destination to arrive at. It is a state of mind, a way of being."

– Desmond Tutu

"Let us not seek to satisfy our thirst for freedom by drinking from the cup of bitterness and hatred."

— Martin Luther King Jr

"All the great things are simple, and many can be expressed in a single word: freedom, justice, honor, duty, mercy, hope." — Winston Churchill

"But laws alone cannot secure freedom of expression; in order that every man may present his views without penalty there must be a spirit of tolerance in the entire population."

— Albert Einstein,

"If you assume that there is an instinct for freedom, there are opportunities to change things, there's a chance you may contribute to making a better world. The choice is yours."

— Noam Chomsky

"Freedom is something that dies unless it's used."

— Hunter S. Thompson

"No one loses anyone, because no one owns anyone. That is the true experience of freedom: having the most important thing in the world without owning it."

— Paulo Coelho

"I've found that there is always some beauty left — in nature, sunshine, freedom, in yourself; these can all help you. Look at these thing, then you find yourself again."

 — Anne Frank, "The Diary of a Young Girl"

"Human kindness has never weakened the stamina or softened the fiber of a free people."

— Franklin D. Roosevelt

"Freedom is not worth having if it does not include the freedom to make mistakes."

– Gandhi

Gandhi's quote, *"Freedom is not worth having if it does not include the freedom to make mistakes,"* resonates deeply and holds significant truth. However, our society has established laws that restrict certain actions, resulting in curtailed freedom and imprisonment for a duration determined by the justice system. It's important to acknowledge that when one's freedom is taken away, it encompasses more than just the legal punishment. The loss of identity and humanity experienced within the illogical and flawed prison system becomes an additional form of punishment.

Authenticity in chaos

Each day behind bars becomes a relentless ordeal, and tragically, many individuals succumb to despair and take their own lives. Serving a prison sentence is no easy feat.

"Prison does not define you. It is what you do with your time inside that can change the trajectory of your life." - Malika Oufkir.

This is true, but many individuals within the system do not have an awareness of this, and the budget-restricted system does not allow the system to offer you a clear trajectory for finding yourself.

While some may argue otherwise, I understand why people might perceive it as easy. For those who desire to evade responsibility, lack purpose, thrive in aggression and turmoil, or lead chaotic lives on the outside, the prison environment may offer an illusion of ease. However, the truth remains that these individuals have likely long strayed from their authentic selves, finding solace in toxic circumstances. *"The true measure of any society can be found in how it treats its most vulnerable members."* - Mahatma Gandhi

It is essential to recognize that the prison experience is a complex and multi-faceted ordeal. It goes beyond the deprivation of physical freedom and delves into the psychological and emotional realms. The loss of freedom is not solely defined by the legal consequences; it encompasses the profound impact on one's sense of self and overall well-being.

"The only way to deal with prison is to redefine it as a place for personal growth and transformation, rather than punishment." - Jack Canfield.

The background that many in the system have puts them in a very disadvantageous position to ever understand Jack Canfield's concept; how can one come to this conclusion when they cannot read or write or suffer from severe childhood trauma that the prison system only fuels rather than negates?

Freedom is crucial to our authenticity because it allows us to fully express our individuality and live in alignment with our true selves. When we have the freedom to make choices, pursue our passions, and determine our own paths, we can explore and embrace our unique identities. Authenticity thrives in an environment where we can be true to our values, beliefs, and desires without external constraints or limitations; unfortunately, this is the exact opposite of what a prison environment offers.

Freedom provides us with the opportunity to discover our passions, interests, and talents. It allows us to explore different experiences, learn from them, and grow as individuals. When we are free to express ourselves authentically, we can cultivate meaningful relationships, pursue fulfilling careers, and engage in activities that resonate with our core being. This is all taken away when we are incarcerated in a toxic atmosphere fuelled by violence and drugs. To survive in prison, we must give up any cultivation of true self and concentrate on surviving and turning our identity into one that will stand up tall in the face of conflict demonisation and stay alive in the dark of hopelessness.

Freedom fosters personal growth and self-awareness. It enables us to reflect on our thoughts, emotions, and experiences, gaining insights into our strengths, weaknesses, and aspirations. Through self-discovery, we can understand our values, set personal goals, and make choices that align with our authentic selves. In prison, we must reflect on how we are to survive, look at strengths and weaknesses that will best suit prison politics, and accept a set of values that is not authentic to our true self, all of which is damaging to personal growth. It must be said that in the fog of lost souls incarcerated, there are those who use the time to find themselves and find the courage to be different; however, these cases are extremely rare and usually come in a theological or spiritual manner, not by the prison system offering a range of ways to become 'authentic.' **To those who managed to do this, I really do take my hat off to you, and it's a feat that should never be underestimated.**

When our freedom is restricted or suppressed, our authenticity can be stifled. External pressures, societal expectations, and constraints imposed by both prisoners and staff can hinder our ability to express who we truly are. In most situations, we conform to societal norms within the prison (otherwise known as prison politics), and we adopt personas to fit in and compromise our values and desires, which leads us ultimately to a sense of disconnection from our true selves.

During my three-year confinement in Shotts, a profound transformation was unfolding within me—an identity shift that I wasn't fully aware of at the time. The relentless grip of prison life had begun to take its toll on my mental well-being and psyche. I found myself growing increasingly resentful of the staff, losing patience with those who couldn't handle the pressures inherent in prison existence. As I became entangled in the web of prison politics, I grew desensitised to the presence of bullying, violence, and drug use, perceiving them as everyday occurrences. Remarkably, this desensitisation extended to long-serving staff members who, over time, succumbed to the inescapable realities of prison life.

It's important to acknowledge that prison officers, due to the nature of their punitive roles, harbor inherent mistrust towards prisoners. This mistrust, I must admit, is not entirely unfounded. By the time individuals find themselves within the hardened walls of HMP Shotts, they have often developed the skills to manipulate and engage in psychological warfare, both with staff and fellow prisoners. The initial years of my sentence were a period of acclimation, a time of learning the ropes of this new identity I had assumed—one characterized by manipulation, self-interest, and survival.

It was during this tumultuous period that I experienced my first anxiety attack. Unaware of what was happening to me, I pressed the emergency bell, fearing I was having a heart attack. After persistent persuasion, nurses eventually attended to me, assessed my condition, and declared that I was physically fine. However, I knew deep within that I wasn't truly fine. My body was signaling a disconnection from my authentic self, alerting me to the chemical imbalances caused by the constant state of hypervigilance and the constant rush of adrenaline and cortisol coursing through me unbeknownst on a daily basis. The values I once held dear in a society that, although inauthentic, I could bear had been lost, and my body was beginning to bear the weight of this transformation.

The impact of imprisonment on my mental health and overall well-being was insidious, silently eroding the foundations of my true self. The strain of constant surveillance and the suppression of my genuine values were taking their toll, manifesting in physical and emotional distress. The prison environment, with its pressures, manipulations, and fractured sense of authenticity, had unwittingly caused a profound rupture within me, which my body was bravely attempting to communicate.

In the midst of the prison's challenging predicament, I encountered diazepam (valium). Diazepam, belonging to the benzodiazepine class of drugs, is a medication frequently prescribed to address various conditions such as anxiety disorders, panic attacks, muscle spasms, and seizures. By enhancing the effects of gamma-aminobutyric acid (GABA), a neurotransmitter in the brain, diazepam promotes relaxation and reduces excessive brain activity. It's an interesting irony to contemplate: relaxation and diminished brain activity within the confines of a prison environment. While some may view this as counterintuitive or illogical, the reality is far more complex.

In a toxic and highly charged environment like a prison, where tensions run high, and stress permeates every aspect of daily life, the appeal of drugs becomes evident. It provides a seemingly logical response to a multi-faceted problem. The allure of a quick solution within such a challenging setting is understandable.

Prisoners are confronted with a myriad of emotions, from fear and anxiety to frustration and despair. The intense environment, with its heightened levels of conflict and animosity, can leave individuals searching for relief from the pressures that surround them. In this context, the allure of substances like diazepam becomes more comprehensible—offering a temporary escape, a respite from the chaos that engulfs their existence.

While the use of drugs in prison may not align with conventional wisdom or societal expectations, it represents an attempt by individuals to find solace amidst the madness. It reflects the innate human desire for relief, however temporary, from the overwhelming challenges of life behind bars. It is within this complex and often contradictory space that we find glimpses of logic in the face of what appears to be madness.

Understanding this reality provides a starting point for addressing the deeper issues within the prison system. By recognizing the underlying motivations and complexities that drive such choices, we can work towards implementing more effective strategies that address the root causes of drug use and promote healthier coping mechanisms. It is through empathy, understanding, and thoughtful interventions that we can navigate the delicate balance between logic and madness within the prison environment.

Valium, as a prescribed and controlled substance, can present significant challenges within a prison environment, and I have seen much violence attributed to this drug in prison. Its effects can lead individuals to experience a false sense of courage, which may manifest as forward aggression. Consequently, the prison system tends to be cautious and reluctant when it comes to distributing Valium. They argue that the potential benefits outweigh the drawbacks, and to some extent, I can understand their perspective. However, it's important to recognize that there is no magical drug that can single-handedly address the profound mental health issues prevalent in prison. The prison is more than happy to distribute drugs like amitriptyline, serequel, mirtazapine, trazodone, etc. These are potent drugs, sometimes anti-psychotic in nature, that hang on you for days, which again can be appealing to a prisoner wanting to block out reality but does little to contribute to true personal growth.

While Valium may provide temporary relief, it carries the risk of addiction and exacerbating existing mental health problems. Moreover, its usage can further distance individuals from their authentic selves. If we focused on the problems of prison life rather than focusing solely on punitive measures, we could strive to better understand the underlying reasons why people turn to drugs in the first place. By embracing a more compassionate and comprehensive approach, we can work towards addressing the root causes of drug use and fostering genuine healing within the prison system.

I must acknowledge that I found myself succumbing to the allure of Valium whenever an opportunity presented itself, eagerly anticipating the next chance to acquire it within the prison walls.

Authenticity in chaos

The temporary relief offered by Valium cannot be underestimated, especially within the harsh prison environment. The extraordinary lengths individuals would go to in order to obtain drugs like Valium further substantiate my claim that no one truly enjoys their time in prison, regardless of the facade they may put on.

The desperation displayed by some prisoners in acquiring drugs is staggering. It reveals the profound impact of imprisonment and the deep-seated desire for any semblance of solace or escape. The lengths individuals go to, including involving family members and risking their loved ones' freedom, utilizing their children or grandparents as unwitting accomplices, and even offering substantial financial incentives to staff members for smuggling, highlight the prominent role that drugs play within the day-to-day operations of the prison system in Scotland.

These desperate measures underscore the undeniable influence and demand for drugs within the prison environment. They reveal the harsh reality that many individuals are willing to risk everything, their own well-being and the well-being of those around them, just to obtain temporary respite from the overwhelming hardships of life behind bars. It is a stark testament to the pervasive challenges faced by prisoners and the profound impact that drugs have within the prison system.

Recognising the pervasiveness of drug use within the prison system is a crucial step toward understanding the complexities at play. It emphasises the pressing need for comprehensive interventions that address not only the supply of drugs but also the underlying factors driving their demand. By exploring alternatives such as increased mental health support rehabilitation programs and addressing the root causes of addiction, we can begin to create a prison environment that prioritises genuine healing and rehabilitation, reducing the reliance on drugs as a coping mechanism.

It is disheartening to observe that the system has not sufficiently learned from past mistakes regarding punitive measures targeting drug addicts. The stark truth is that **"YOU CANNOT PUNISH ADDICTION OUT OF SOMEONE."** Despite the passage of time since my own incarceration in 2005, the system has made minimal progress in this regard. Our prisons continue to be inundated with substances that were not even known back then, substances far more dangerous and potent. Drugs like etizolam and spice have become alarmingly common within the Scottish prison system. The rapid evolution of chemical compounds within these substances makes it nearly impossible for drug tests to keep up with technological advancements.

It is disheartening to hear numerous staff members express sentiments such as, "I would bring back the old drugs in a heartbeat." This statement underscores the profound frustration and disillusionment caused by the system's attempt to use punitive measures to eradicate drugs like heroin, hash, and valium from the lives of addicts. Rather than addressing the root causes of addiction and providing effective support, the punitive approach has only perpetuated a cycle of struggle and frustration.

To break this cycle, it is essential that we shift our focus towards comprehensive strategies that prioritize addiction treatment, mental health support, and addressing the underlying factors that contribute to substance abuse. By acknowledging the limitations of punitive measures and embracing more empathetic and evidence-based approaches, we can pave the way for meaningful change within the prison system. The aim should be to foster an environment that genuinely supports individuals in their journey towards recovery, reducing the allure and reliance on drugs as a means of escape. Unfortunately, until the Scottish government makes radical changes within the system, the inescapable truth is inevitable, and the prison system will continue to churn out hate-fuelled, drug-addicted, and traumatised souls; *"God bless all the lost souls, and may they find peace one day."*

My time in Shotts prison was a profound lesson in the art of imprisonment. It taught me how to live, behave, and even speak like a prisoner. Inside those walls, we were compelled to put on an act, transforming ourselves into a crude, toxic, and distorted version of our authentic selves sculpted by the prison environment. In this realm, even acts of kindness among fellow prisoners were viewed with suspicion and labeled as an *"angle"* or hidden agenda.

As human beings, kindness towards one another is a natural inclination ingrained within us. Yet, within the prison system, this authenticity is overshadowed by the need to survive. It reminds me of the fascinating example of hunter-gatherer societies. In these societies, individuals coexist and cooperate despite lacking blood ties. They readily share resources and collaborate in hunting, fishing, and gathering food. Why is this the case?

Survival hinges on sharing and cooperation, as emphasised by Andrea Migliano, the senior author of a notable study. Although hunters may only succeed in finding food around 75 percent of the time, the presence of unrelated neighbors ensures that no family goes hungry one day out of four. These tribes have evolved mechanisms to foster cooperation with individuals who are not genetically related.

Reducing the number of kin within a camp also yields an unexpected benefit. It creates a network where individuals likely have relatives scattered among different camps. These familial connections facilitate bonding and the exchange of crucial information and tools. Instead of resorting to force or transactions, the tribes establish connections, strengthening their collective resilience.

In both the prison system and the hunter-gatherer societies, the act of adapting, altering our natural inclinations, becomes a means of survival. While prisoners conform to a distorted version of themselves, the tribes learn to cooperate with unrelated individuals, recognising the advantages of a broader network and shared resources. It is a testament to the remarkable adaptability of human beings in the face of challenging circumstances, transcending the boundaries of kinship to forge connections that enable collective progress.

Unfortunately, this authentic hunter-gatherer kindness that we have as an inherent trait is a trait that is seen as a weakness in prison, and therefore, you must learn that kindness can quickly become a factor for bullying, aggressiveness, passive-aggressive behaviors, violence, etc., by other prisoners. We can only be what our environment allows us to be, and there are people who experience prison life for six months in a cushy position and think they can become advocates for people who are long-term prisoners; I can safely say well over 90 percent, I personally would say 100 percent, with some able to put on a better front than others, but a good front does not allow us to heal or become the true authentic person we were supposed to be, most of these people find themselves embroiled in a life of organized crime or chaotic addiction; usually one of these two factors are at play with anyone who has served a significant amount of time in prison.

When I speak of doing time, I mean anyone who has spent four years or more behind bars and had to mold to survive the mental and mindful onslaught that our environment has created for us. I can say with a large degree of certainty that if a study was commissioned and the true facts were to come to light, there would be a full diagnosis of PTSD for all prisoners and staff who have lived in this madness. How anyone can take a look at the prison system and believe that this model is doing its best to rehabilitate prisoners is beyond me; the current model is so far from rehabilitating anyone it is hard to even draw a comparison. The Oxford Dictionary describes rehabilitation as:

"Definition of rehabilitation noun from the Oxford Advanced Learner's Dictionary rehabilitation noun /ˌriːəˌbɪlɪteɪʃn/ /ˌriːəˌbɪlɪteɪʃn/ [uncountable] the process of helping somebody to return to a normal, healthy life after they have been in prison or very ill."

Chapter Five: Rehabilitation: Myth or Reality? Uncovering the Truth and Advocating for Change

The struggle to combat the deeply flawed prison system is a reality I confront regularly in my work. I encounter individuals who have been abruptly released from prison, left with nothing—no home, no money, no family, and no support. They arrive, burdened by drug addiction, unaware of any concept of rehabilitation; rehabilitation is but a pipe dream to these people. Upon release, they turn to third-sector charity organizations for assistance. In these moments of crisis, places like Phoenix Futures, SISCO and Turning Point become invaluable lifelines for these individuals.

Operating within an extremely constrained budget, the prison system cannot bear the sole responsibility for its abysmal rehabilitation success rate. However, it is essential for them to speak up honestly about the deplorable state in which our prison system finds itself. They cannot hide behind the manipulated statistics they present annually to the public and the government. Even when doctored, these statistics paint a bleak picture for any institution. While the prison system is not entirely to blame—*(they cannot fully attend to the complex needs of each individual prisoner)*—they must not perpetuate an inauthentic image to the public. This false portrayal convinces the public and the government that a rehabilitative system exists, one that upholds authentic and positive values. The truth is far from that. It never has been.

The cycle of traumatising both the incarcerated population and the workers within the system continues unabated. We persist in demonising the behaviors of a traumatised and vulnerable sector of society. Yet, we most probably acknowledge that the system, from childhood onwards, has repeatedly failed these individuals. Until one of our own, someone close to us is directly affected, it is easy to believe the distorted version that the Scottish Prison Service (SPS) and the government present.

Pause for a moment and think about that person in your life who has been let down by the system. We all know someone who struggles, grappling with complex addiction or mental health issues. Astonishingly, that person we know represents a significant majority of the prison population. As we read the sensationalised narratives in tabloid newspapers or listen to the news each day, let us remember that person in our lives.

It may lead us to conclude that they deserve to be confined within those walls. However, if even a glimmer of doubt arises, suggesting these individuals are victims of society's norms, then we can begin to sow the seeds for real and lasting change. The change will genuinely benefit our prison population and society as a whole, as our prisoners are released with a much better chance of living a pro-social life where they can be productive and valuable members of society. There are many cases of prisoners going on to do wonderful things:

- *Georgia Durante was a getaway driver for the Mafia before starting a stunt-driving company.*

- *Duncan Bannatyne was a prisoner before becoming a hugely successful businessman.*

- *Frank William Abagnale was a world-famous con man by age 21. Now, he runs a fraud consulting company.*

- *Kweisi Mfume had several stints in jail before becoming a Congressman and serving as president of the NAACP.*

- *Junior Johnson went to jail for smuggling alcohol before becoming a NASCAR driver.*

- *Former Nixon aide Charles Colson spent a year in federal prison for his involvement in the Watergate scandal and then started Prison Fellowship.*

- *Larry Jay Levine was sentenced to 10 years in prison and later used his experience to start his company, 'Wall Street Prison Consultants'*

- *Judge Greg Mathis was in a gang and served time before launching his own TV show.*

- *Actor Danny Trejo spent 12 years robbing stores, but now he only plays 'the bad guy' in movies.*

- *Stephen Richards spent nine years in prison for selling marijuana before becoming a professor of criminal justice.*

- *Fyodor Dostoevsky - The Russian novelist and philosopher famous for works such as "Crime and Punishment" and "The Brothers Karamazov," was sentenced to four years of hard labor in a Siberian prison camp.*

- *Mark Wahlberg - The actor, producer, and businessman known for his roles in films such as "The Departed" and "Ted," had a troubled youth that involved criminal activities and a prison sentence.*

What do these people say about prison?

Georgia Durante, a former model and stunt driver, has shared her experiences and reflections on prison in her autobiography titled "The Company She Keeps." In her book, she discusses her involvement in organized crime, her arrest, and subsequent time spent in prison. Here are some general themes and perspectives she has expressed about prison:

- **Personal Growth and Reflection:** Durante has discussed how her time in prison allowed her to reflect on her choices, confront the consequences of her actions, and ultimately find the motivation to change her life for the better.

- **Rehabilitation and Second Chances:** Durante has emphasised the importance of rehabilitation and second chances, sharing her belief that individuals who have been incarcerated should have the opportunity to reform, reintegrate into society, and pursue a positive path.

- **Impact on Mental and Emotional Well-being:** Durante has highlighted the challenges and emotional toll that incarceration can have on individuals, including the loss of freedom, separation from loved ones, and the need to navigate a complex prison environment.

- **Advocacy for Criminal Justice Reform:** Durante has become an advocate for criminal justice reform, speaking out about the need for fair sentencing, access to rehabilitation programs, and support systems to help individuals successfully transition back into society after serving their sentences.

These points offer a general overview of some of Georgia Durante's perspectives and what she has shared about her experiences within prison. For more specific insights, I would recommend referring to her autobiography, ***"The Company She Keeps."***

Frank Abagnale, the former con artist turned security consultant, has shared some insights about his time in prison in various interviews and his autobiography, "Catch Me If You Can." Here are a few notable quotes and themes related to his prison experience:

- "I was confined for almost five years, and I can assure you that without exception, no one wants to be incarcerated. It's a very lonely, difficult, and often brutal existence."

- Abagnale has described the challenges of adjusting to the harsh realities of prison life, including the loss of freedom, restricted personal space, and the constant need to be vigilant for personal safety.

- "During my time in prison, I realized the true consequences of my actions and the harm I caused to others. It was a humbling experience that made me genuinely remorseful for the crimes I had committed."

- Abagnale has emphasised the importance of personal growth and self-reflection during his incarceration. He used the time to educate himself, develop new skills, and plan for a different future.

- "Prison taught me the value of integrity and living an honest life. I made a promise to myself that I would never go back to my old ways and that I would use my experiences to help others."

Abagnale's reflections on his time in prison demonstrate his transformation and the insights he gained from that experience. He has become an advocate for ethical behavior and fraud prevention, using his past as a cautionary tale and a source of inspiration for positive change.

Danny Trejo: Danny Trejo's time in prison was a challenging and traumatic experience for him. He has described it as a **"living hell,"**

with violence, fear, and loneliness being constant companions. The harsh environment of prison subjected him to terrible acts of violence, including stabbings and gang fights.

Mark Wahlberg: In 2016, Mark Wahlberg admitted that there was a time in his life when he looked at going to prison as some sort of accomplishment — an end game, if you will, to his life of juvenile crime. Indeed, as Distractify reports, he admitted that once he was locked up, he was with the types of guys that he wanted to be. Unfortunately, prison wasn't the experience he thought it was going to be. "I realised it wasn't what I wanted at all. I'd ended up in the worst place I could possibly imagine, and I never wanted to go back," he said. Read More: https://www.grunge.com/658375/what-mark-wahlbergs-life-in-prison-was-really-like/

Fyodor Dostoevsky, the renowned Russian novelist, expressed profound insights about prison life based on his personal experiences. In his novel "The House of the Dead" and other writings, he delves into the psychological and social dynamics of the prison environment. Here are a few notable quotes attributed to Dostoevsky regarding prison life:

- "The degree of civilization in a society can be judged by entering its prisons." This quote highlights Dostoevsky's belief that the treatment of prisoners reflects the moral and societal development of a civilization.

- "The degree of civilization in a society can be judged by entering its prisons." Dostoevsky emphasizes the transformative potential of prison, where individuals confront their own flaws, reflect on their actions, and seek redemption.

- "The degree of civilization in a society can be judged by entering its prisons." Dostoevsky underscores the importance of empathy and compassion in society, urging readers to view prisoners not just as criminals but as individuals capable of growth and redemption.

- "The degree of civilization in a society can be judged by entering its prisons." This quote also suggests that the prison system should focus on rehabilitation and reform rather than solely punitive measures. Dostoevsky advocates for the idea that prisons should strive to reintegrate individuals back into society as changed and rehabilitated individuals.

- Dostoevsky's writings on prison life offer profound insights into the human condition, highlighting the potential for transformation, the need for compassion, and the complex dynamics within the prison environment.

Charles Colson, the former aide to President Richard Nixon, had a notable experience of prison life. After his involvement in the Watergate scandal, Colson was convicted of obstruction of justice and served seven months in federal prison. During and after his time in prison, Colson underwent a significant personal transformation that led him to dedicate his life to prison ministry and criminal justice reform. Here are a few key aspects of his prison experience and subsequent reflections:

- **Spiritual Awakening:** Colson's time in prison played a pivotal role in his spiritual journey. He described his experience as a "born-again" moment that led him to embrace Christianity and profoundly changed the trajectory of his life.

- **Empathy for Prisoners:** Colson's firsthand exposure to the realities of prison life and the challenges faced by incarcerated individuals fostered a deep empathy within him. He recognised the need for prison reform and sought to advocate for better conditions and opportunities for prisoners.

- **Prison Fellowship:** Inspired by his own transformation and driven by a desire to help others, Colson founded Prison Fellowship, a nonprofit organization dedicated to supporting prisoners, ex-prisoners, and their families. The organization provides various programs and resources aimed at rehabilitation, reintegration, and fostering personal and spiritual growth.

- **Criminal Justice Reform:** Colson became a prominent advocate for criminal justice reform, calling for a more restorative approach that emphasizes rehabilitation and addressing the root causes of crime. He highlighted the importance of education, job training, and community support in reducing recidivism rates.

- **Authorship and Speaking Engagements:** Colson wrote several books based on his experiences, including "Born Again" and "Loving God," which detail his spiritual journey and the impact of his prison experience. He also traveled extensively as a public speaker, sharing his insights on faith, redemption, and criminal justice reform.

Charles Colson's prison experience was a turning point in his life, leading him to devote his energy and influence to advocating for prisoners and promoting meaningful reform within the criminal justice system. His story serves as an example of personal transformation and the potential for positive change, both for individuals who have been incarcerated and for society as a whole.

Larry Jay Levine, a former federal inmate and founder of Wall Street Prison Consultants, has shared insights and perspectives on prison life based on his personal experiences. He has also provided guidance and support to individuals facing incarceration. Here are some general themes and perspectives that Levine has expressed regarding prison life:

- **Navigating the Prison Environment:** Levine has provided advice on how to adapt to the prison environment, including tips on staying safe, managing relationships with other inmates, and understanding the unwritten rules and dynamics within prison walls.

- **Coping with Isolation and Separation:** Levine has addressed the emotional and psychological challenges that individuals face while being separated from their loved ones and the outside world. He has shared strategies for maintaining relationships and dealing with the sense of isolation that can accompany incarceration.

- **Utilizing Resources and Programs:** Levine has emphasized the importance of taking advantage of available resources and programs within the prison system. This includes participating in educational opportunities, vocational training, and mental health support services to enhance personal growth and prepare for reentry.

- **Understanding Legal Rights and Processes:** Levine has provided insights on navigating the legal aspects of the prison system, including understanding one's rights, appealing convictions, and accessing legal resources to ensure a fair process.

Authenticity in chaos

- **Preparing for Reentry:** Levine has focused on the importance of preparing for life after prison, offering guidance on job prospects, building a support network, and making a successful transition back into society.

Larry Jay Levine's expertise stems from his personal experiences as well as his work as a consultant, assisting individuals facing incarceration. His perspectives provide practical advice and insights for those entering or currently in the prison system, helping them better navigate the challenges they may encounter.

The ex-prisoners mentioned above share a common starting point: a level of awareness and intelligence that sets them apart from many incarcerated individuals worldwide, not just in Scotland. It's unfortunate that a significant number of prisoners lack basic literacy skills, struggling to read or write. While prisons do offer classes to teach these skills, attendance is often low due to the stigma attached to being an adult in a class for reading and writing. In an environment choked by egos, revealing one's inability to read or write is seen unfavorably, carrying a certain stigma that prisoners are hesitant to expose.

Moreover, promising initiatives like peer mentoring and tutoring often face obstacles due to incidents that violate prison rules, such as the unauthorised transfer of drugs between cell blocks. While it's important to address such misconduct and hold individuals accountable, it's disheartening that these incidents can derail potentially positive projects. The prison security team tends to label such initiatives as security risks, impeding their progress. Navigating these complexities is undoubtedly a challenging task for prison officials, and I don't envy their predicament. However, it is essential to prioritise common sense and exercise discernment in prisons. It's unfair to shut down entire projects due to the actions of a single person. As the saying goes in Scotland, which holds true in a prison setting, *"you fly with the crows, you get shot with the crows."*

It is important to recognise that the notion of *"we believe people can change"* is not a mere value or a superficial attempt by the prison system to present itself as forward-thinking. This perspective is grounded in the reality that countless individuals have demonstrated the capacity for personal growth and transformation, even in the face of adversity. The successes mentioned earlier serve as powerful examples of individuals who have overcome their pasts and achieved remarkable accomplishments.

To dismiss the belief in people's capacity to change as trivial or insignificant is shortsighted. The evidence of personal growth and transformation is abundant, extending far beyond the cases mentioned earlier. Countless individuals, both within and outside the prison system, have managed to turn their lives around, break free from destructive patterns, and contribute positively to society.

It is crucial to acknowledge that change is not a matter of debate but an inherent truth backed by extensive research and personal experiences. By embracing the belief that people can change, the prison system recognises the potential for rehabilitation and seeks to provide individuals with the support and opportunities necessary for their transformation.

In addition to believing in change, the prison system could offer a range of valuable resources and programs to support individuals in their transformation and prepare them for successful reintegration into society. It is not hard to come up with a quick summary of what prisoners need:

- *Comprehensive Rehabilitation Programs: Implementing well-designed and evidence-based programs that address various aspects of an individual's life, such as education, vocational training, life skills development, and anger management. These programs should be tailored to meet the specific needs of each person, focusing on their strengths and interests.*

- *Education and Skill Development: Providing access to quality education programs, including literacy courses, GED programs, vocational training, and higher education opportunities. Equipping individuals with marketable skills increases their chances of finding meaningful employment upon release.*

- *Mental Health Services: Recognizing the importance of mental health support, offering comprehensive mental health assessments, counseling, and therapy to address underlying issues and promote psychological well-being. Collaboration with mental health professionals and ensuring continuity of care during and after incarceration is crucial.*

- *Substance Abuse Treatment: Developing specialised programs that address substance abuse issues, including counseling, detoxification, and rehabilitation services. Combining medical and therapeutic approaches can help individuals overcome addiction and develop healthy coping strategies.*

- *Restorative Justice Programs: Implementing restorative justice initiatives that emphasise repairing harm, promoting accountability, and rebuilding relationships between offenders and victims. This can involve mediation, victim-offender dialogues, and community service, fostering understanding and reconciliation.*

- *Transitional Support: Establishing comprehensive reentry programs that offer support before, during, and after release. This may include assistance with housing, employment, financial management, and connecting individuals with community-based organisations that provide ongoing support and guidance.*

- *Family and Social Support: Recognising the importance of maintaining healthy relationships and facilitating regular communication between incarcerated individuals and their families through visitation programs, family counseling, and support groups. Strengthening family ties can be instrumental in successful reintegration.*

- *Community Engagement and Integration: Encouraging partnerships between prisons and community organisations to promote volunteer work, skill-building opportunities, and community-based programs. This fosters a sense of belonging and helps individuals develop a positive identity outside of the prison environment.*

The presence of support and positive examples within prisons is not entirely absent, but it is undoubtedly limited. There exists a significant void in the extent of support that can be provided, and unfortunately, only a small fraction of individuals within the prison system possess the necessary mindset for such examples to truly make a difference. It is crucial to acknowledge that few prisoners have access to a positive support network that can offer guidance and stability upon their release.

Many of the examples provided earlier rely on prisoners having the desire to change and being aware of the need to confront and challenge their authentic selves. Regrettably, this awareness and

Authenticity in chaos

motivation for transformation are rare among inmates, leading them to remain trapped in the destructive cycle of criminality and chaos.

This disconnect from authenticity perpetuates a vicious cycle, hindering the effectiveness of the support and examples available. It is essential to recognise the significant barriers that prevent individuals from embracing change and seeking the support they require to break free from destructive patterns. We must remember the walls we build as prisoners and how much we live in survival mode, a mode that is not easy to switch off. This hyper-vigilant state can keep us in **'fight or flight mode,'** resisting the path to our true selves.

Addressing this issue calls for a multi-faceted approach that not only provides support but also fosters the necessary mindset and self-awareness within the prison population. It requires interventions that can effectively reach individuals who may not initially recognise the need for change, helping them reconnect with their authentic selves and empowering them to make positive choices.

By acknowledging these challenges and striving for innovative solutions, we can work towards bridging the gap in support within the prison system. By addressing the underlying issues that hinder prisoners' receptiveness to change and providing comprehensive resources tailored to their specific needs, we can enhance the chances of successful rehabilitation and reintegration into society.

By offering these comprehensive resources and programs, the prison system can create an environment that not only believes in change but actively facilitates and nurtures it. These initiatives empower individuals to acquire the necessary skills, support systems, and mindset to lead productive lives upon release, reducing recidivism and promoting positive outcomes for both individuals and society as a whole.

While the prison system may face significant challenges and limitations, recognising the potential for change is essential for cultivating a rehabilitative environment. Believing in the capacity for transformation not only offers hope to individuals within the system but also contributes to the overall goal of reducing reoffending rates and promoting a more positive and productive society.

Therefore, it is misguided to dismiss the value of believing in people's ability to change. Instead, we should strive to create a system that truly embraces this belief and supports individuals in their journey toward personal growth and reintegration into society. Consider, for a moment, that we could all find ourselves in a position where we or our loved ones could be incarcerated. How would you want to be treated? How would you want your son, daughter, father, or mother to be treated within the system? Ponder this deeply, and you will realise that no one desires for them to emerge from prison in a more negative and deteriorated state than when they entered. Sadly, this is the harsh reality we face. It will persist until we bring about change or concede that prison is a dead-end for many individuals, effectively writing them off. But then, can we be surprised or angry at the behaviours prisoners' exhibit once they are set free?

This is a difficult and contentious topic, even among prison staff. Some advocate for providing prisoners with nothing more than bread and water, while others yearn for a more therapeutic and rehabilitative environment. The opinions are divided, reflecting the complexity and controversy surrounding the issue. However, until we address these systemic challenges and embrace a more compassionate approach, the cycle of suffering and recidivism will persist. We must confront these difficult truths and work toward a prison system that genuinely fosters rehabilitation and positive transformation.

Authenticity in chaos

As my three-year tenure in Shotts drew to a close, whispers began circulating about the new establishment on the horizon. HMP Addiewell, a privately-run prison located in West Lothian, was set to open its doors, accommodating inmates primarily from the Lanarkshire region—myself included. The anticipated transition was penciled in for the winter of 2009.

The news of my impending transfer to HMP Addiewell was a monumental development, a game-changing twist that promised an entirely different tempest of turmoil and uncertainty. The prospect of entering this new facility brought with it a hurricane of chaos, a fresh chapter in my prison journey that held both anticipation and trepidation.

Chapter Six: Inside HMP Addiewell: The Vortex of Addiction, Chaos, and the Dual Diagnosis Battle

HMP Addiewell, a state-of-the-art prison facility, was constructed in 2009 within Scotland's West Lothian region. Its establishment aimed to address the surging prison population in Scotland by accommodating both local West Lothian inmates and those from Lanarkshire. Given that I hail from Cumbernauld in North Lanarkshire, I fell within the jurisdiction and was informed by Shotts staff that I would be among the initial group of inmates transferring to this innovative institution. Initially, the prison received 12 individuals from HMP Shotts and another 12 from HMP Glenochil. As we embarked on our journey to the new facility, anticipation and curiosity consumed us, eager to experience the modernity and design of this recently constructed prison and listening to stories about the farce of the opening of HMP Kilmarnock, we were all of the views we would see how much we could get away with and push the boundaries.

Upon our arrival, the prison staff surpassed our expectations. A line of eager prison officers warmly greeted us, creating a surreal atmosphere. This transfer differed greatly from previous experiences of being moved between prisons or attending court hearings or hospital visits. As we approached the Reliance van, the prisoners inside erupted into song, rocking the vehicle and leaving the staff visibly unsettled. Understandably, this unique event marked their first encounter with prisoners, and for many of the staff, it marked the beginning of a new career.

We were individually escorted out of the van and processed with surprising friendliness. It was an unconditioned approach, as the staff had never worked with prisoners before; therefore, there was no conditioned mindset from the staff. Even though the prison was under the authority of the SPS and they had received training, their lack of experience in dealing with seasoned and hardened criminals who had navigated the system for years became evident. Among the initial group sent to Addiewell, there were some seasoned characters whose presence would manifest in various ways. In fact, during the first couple of years, you could say the prisoners played a significant role in running the prison to some extent. This took on different forms, and as with any new establishment, scandals and situations arose that were frankly unimaginable to me as a prisoner, never mind being a brand new staff member who had never experienced prison and its undercurrent of anti-social and anti-authority behavior.

During processing, the staff surprised us by offering Mars bars and other confectionery, along with cartons of fruit juice. It was a departure from the typical atmosphere one would expect upon arriving at a prison. Normally, when entering a new jail for the first time, the reception area is usually bustling with activity and serves as the central hub for daily operations. The staff usually make it a point to assert their authority. However, Addiewell presented a different scene, a more friendly scene, a more *'authentic'* human being to human being interaction. Whether this would be taken advantage of in the near future was irrelevant at that time; humans' natural nature was to be kind and pleasant. Of course, this is the prison we are talking about, and this would not last, but it was a nice change, and I can remember it being a much more pleasant experience than other prisons.

The processing of the prisoners followed a similar pattern, but the security checks conducted were not as stringent as those in other prisons. In fact, we were fortunate enough to bring in items that would have been prohibited in most other establishments. To be

78

fair, Shotts, where we came from, had a somewhat relaxed attitude towards such matters, although they would have thoroughly inspected anything before allowing it inside.

Prisoners possess a knack for cleverly smuggling contraband into the prisons, and much of what I've witnessed being brought in would be incredibly difficult to detect and border on genuinely well-thought-out, strategic, and all-round ingenious plans.

One by one, we were escorted to the new cell blocks, where each of us was assigned a cell that would become our home for many years to come. The cells were very clean and boasted showers in them, something that I had never witnessed in the previous prisons I was in, and I remember the papers making a huge deal out of the fact that we had showers in our cells and that we had flat-screen TVs, etc. I can assure you that most of the time, the shower was a treacle and was often freezing cold, and the TVs might have been a flat screen, but they were a make I had genuinely never heard of, and they were very small in size; it's not that I'm suggesting they were inadequate for a prison, certainly not, but they undoubtedly did not match the lavishness the media tried to portray. The exaggerated narrative created by the papers and media only fuels the debates that lack substance and keep us from making true and positive steps toward a better prison community.

While this book primarily focuses on the impossibility of being one's *authentic* self within the prison, some events within the notorious walls of HMP Addiewell are worth sharing to note the skills that prisoners possess and the unnatural conditions we can find ourselves in when confined behind prison walls. From its inception, Addiewell aimed to be an educational prison, challenging the conventional and purposeless activities that typically dominate prison institutions. These activities, referred to

Authenticity in chaos

as *"sheds,"* encompass various opportunities for prisoners during their incarceration.

For instance, there was a wood shop shed where skilled individuals could channel their craftsmanship and build impressive creations from wood. Personally, I was more inclined towards education and writing rather than working with tools, so the sheds weren't my forte. However, for many, the sheds became a vital part of their daily routine, enabling them to express their creativity and find an outlet for their skills. I have witnessed remarkable feats of ingenuity when building contraband hiding spots, otherwise known as *'stashes,'* constructed within these sheds, so elaborate that they could astound even the CIA and MI5, "let alone a prison security team." I have heard of prisoners making papier-mâché still saws and stealing the original to try and break free. I have seen doll houses that would be worth thousands on the outside, lavish benches, and many more very impressive works of art by prisoners. Yet, on the other hand, the sheds also served as gathering places for individuals to simply sit, enjoy a cup of coffee, and engage in wild criminal conversations. These discussions perpetuated a certain mindset, fostering alliances that often extended beyond their time behind bars. Therefore, while my personal story may not take center stage, it is imperative to shed light on these distinctive aspects of life within HMP Addiewell.

Addiewell opened its doors, and from the very beginning, the environment felt starkly different. The staff exhibited a sense of naivety, often falling victim to prisoners' mind games and learning manipulative behaviors. It's crucial not to criticise the Addiewell staff, as many genuinely aimed to make a positive impact on the lives of these lost souls within the prison system. However, they were ill-prepared for the onslaught of manipulative tactics and the deceptive personas adopted by certain prisoners who essentially controlled the day-to-day operations of the prison.

An incident that was both amusing and deeply unsettling showcased the staff's alarming naivety when Addiewell first opened. It began when an inmate inquired about the annual Christmas disco at HMP Cortonvale, a female prison in Scotland at the time. Instead of dismissing the question, the staff member decided to investigate and started walking around the hall, gathering names for the disco. He even shouted at his colleague, suggesting they might need more than one van to transport the attendees. This bizarre situation persisted until he approached the hall manager with the list of names. Later, he returned to us, saying, "That was out of order, guys, I got my baws kicked for that there."

These incidents, despite the humorous undertone, revealed a disconcerting level of naivety that deeply affected our sense of safety. Addiewell is a maximum-security prison where inmates have numerous enemies, and violence is a constant threat. The fact that the staff fell for such a foolish prank raised significant concerns about their ability to ensure our well-being. Similar incidents were frequent during the early days of Addiewell, eroding our confidence in the prison as a secure environment. The unsettling truth is that experiences like this can undermine our psychological safety mechanisms, leaving us vulnerable and uncertain in an already challenging setting.

Staff members frequently turned to prisoners for guidance, resulting in the dissemination of incorrect information for personal gain. A notable example of this occurred when we heard about drug smuggling taking place at HMP Kilmarnock, Scotland's first private prison. People were receiving drugs concealed within their mail, as the staff in Kilmarnock failed to inspect the incoming letters, simply tossing them onto the pool tables and allowing prisoners to handle their own mail. Consequently, when the staff at Addiewell sought advice on mail distribution, prisoners recommended replicating the practices from Kilmarnock. This led to several months of prisoners easily obtaining drugs sent through the mail, ranging from powdered benzodiazepines, cocaine, and heroin to intricately crafted cannabis pieces. Paintings disguised as children's drawings arrived, their paint laced with valium, causing prisoners to consume the drug-laden paper.

This lax approach created an environment where drugs were readily available, posing significant risks to both prisoners and staff. The subsequent months witnessed a surge in violence, exacerbated by a shortage of staff as many resigned or took leave due to anxiety and depression. Some staff members were driven solely by personal gain caught smuggling alcohol into the prison in exchange for money. I had a surreal encounter when a prison officer openly entered my cell, offering me a mobile phone in exchange for £500. I declined but later discovered that he had successfully smuggled in numerous phones. Eventually, he was caught with a phone on the premises and subsequently dismissed from his position.

Understandably, the educational opportunities within the prison were largely overlooked by the majority of the inmate population as word spread about the seemingly easy lifestyle Addiewell offered. However, this illusion of comfort came at a high cost, as violence and an overall sense of insecurity permeated the facility. The once-coveted freedom to choose any hall accompanied by a staff member was swiftly abandoned after a prisoner fell victim to a violent attack orchestrated by an adversary from a different hall. It was an environment akin to hell on earth, where an overwhelming feeling of unsafety prevailed. The sad thing is that in 2023, HMP Addiewell seems to be the worst it has ever been, I cannot say this with any experience but I am told by reliable sources that overall it is a lot worse than when I was there in 2009 or 2019, which is scary to say the least.

In this chaotic setting, hypervigilance became a survival instinct. Many of us turned to medications as a means to numb the pain of existence in such a harsh environment. I personally became addicted to painkillers, such as tramadol and codeine, using them as a means of escape rather than for their intended purpose of alleviating physical discomfort. Drugs like diazepam and zopiclone provided solace, allowing for temporary oblivion from the harsh reality surrounding us.

The initial phase of Addiewell's existence was marked by a treacherous and unsafe atmosphere despite some positive aspects. We, the prisoners, had no choice but to adapt swiftly to our surroundings or risk being consumed by the relentless state of affairs. It was during this period that hypervigilance took hold, medication became a refuge, and the desire to escape the painful reality intensified.

The prison environment I experienced provided the perfect breeding ground for what is known as *"dual diagnosis,"* a term that the prison system had long despised and still had done upon my release in 2020. But what exactly does dual diagnosis entail? In essence, it represents the intricate entwinement of substance abuse and mental health issues. Allow me to elaborate on this phenomenon through a comprehensive example:

1. *A person's mental health undergoes a decline due to circumstances that deviate from their "authentic self." This decline can be triggered by a wide range of factors, ranging from a major traumatic event to a surge in anxiety resulting from life's hardships.*

2. *Seeking solace, the individual turns to a substance that offers respite, temporarily numbing the pain they wish to escape in their life. This substance serves as a coping mechanism, whether the underlying cause is significant, such as childhood abuse, or seemingly trivial, such as despising one's job.*

3. *The chosen substance provides a temporary escape from the root problem that caused the decline in mental health. By alleviating emotional pain or undesirable feelings, the individual develops a logical interest in continuing its use.*

4. *As the substance is consumed more frequently, it becomes a defense mechanism, shielding the individual from the unwanted emotions and feelings they were initially experiencing.*

5. *Continued and increased consumption of the drug leads to the body developing a tolerance, necessitating higher and more regular dosages to achieve the desired numbing effect.*

6. *Eventually, addiction takes hold. The individual finds themselves trapped in a cycle where they now have both an addiction and a mental health problem that are inherently intertwined. The pain from the initial emotional distress persists, while the addiction compounds the complexity of their situation.*

Should the mental health problem worsen, the individual resorts to consuming more of the substance as a means of self-medication. Alternatively, if they attempt to eradicate the substance from their lives, the original mental health issue remains, often exacerbated by the symptoms of withdrawal.

This interplay between substance abuse and mental health issues, known as dual diagnosis, creates a complex and challenging scenario for individuals affected by it. Breaking free from this cycle requires specialized and comprehensive support that addresses both the addiction and the underlying mental health concerns.

Throughout my time in Addiewell, I found myself caught up in the never-ending cycle of court hearings and appeals. These legal proceedings not only took a toll on me and my family but also deeply affected the victims' families. Seeking help for my deteriorating mental health, I turned to the doctor, desperate for relief. However, each time I approached him, I was met with the disheartening response that he had no power to alleviate my suffering, as it lay within the realm of the judicial system.

By that point, my body was already reliant on potent painkillers like tramadol, prescribed to manage a back injury I had sustained in HMP Shotts while weightlifting. Additionally, I was taking strong sleeping tablets called zopiclone, which shared similarities with benzodiazepines. The doctor had also attempted various antidepressants, serequel, and mirtazapine. Unbeknownst to me, I began to depend on these substances to numb the daily pain I experienced. I relied on the other medications to find solace in sleep and escape the relentless thoughts plaguing my mind.

Unaware of the potential consequences, I continued down this treacherous path, spiraling into the dark realms of addiction. Little did I realise that I had become entangled in the grips of substance reliance. Unwittingly, I found myself in a constant state of fight-or-flight, battling both the appeal hearings and the daily survival mode of prison life. Addiewell, with its chaotic atmosphere, exacerbated these struggles, pushing me further into the depths of despair.

Authenticity in chaos

Addiction can be an incredibly lonely and isolating experience, especially within the confines of a prison environment. Behind bars, the already limited support network available on the outside becomes even scarcer. The close-knit relationships and bonds that could potentially provide solace and understanding are often fractured or non-existent within the prison community.

In the midst of addiction, the focus narrows down to the constant pursuit of the substance, leading to a withdrawal from social interactions. Friends and acquaintances may distance themselves, either due to their own struggles or the fear of being associated with someone caught in the grip of addiction. The stigma attached to substance abuse can further intensify the isolation, making it challenging to find empathy or companionship among fellow inmates. The vast majority of inmates are struggling with severe mental health and addiction problems and their sole purpose for the day is to find a substance, sometimes any substance, to escape their own minds. Addiction can unfortunately make us selfish, and this behaviour, although necessary and logical to you at the time, further isolates you from your authentic self and authentic relationships, both inside and out, leading to a further disconnect from true reality.

Chapter Seven: The Prison of the Mind: ACES, Escapism, and the Battle for Mental Freedom

'Escapism', if you try and think rationally and imagine yourself in prison, where every fiber of your body wants to escape the harsh reality you find yourself in, then drugs do become a logical option.

The chaotic and nerve-racking setting, along with the unnatural environment, consumes you psychologically and often physically, in turn creating the perfect breeding ground for dual-diagnosed addicts. Escapism becomes a logical inclination within the challenging and often oppressive environment of prison. The daily reality of incarceration, with its limited freedoms, rigid routines, and constant reminders of one's loss of autonomy, can be overwhelming.

Drugs play a significant role in providing a form of escape within the prison context. Drugs play a significant role in prison reality as a whole; it is at the heart of most of the violence and is so wired into prison politics. It cannot be understated how much drugs play an essential role in the day-to-day dealings of prison life. Substance abuse offers a respite from the monotony, boredom, and emotional distress that often accompany long periods of confinement. Unfortunately, drugs can become your best friend in prison and offer you everything you need to find peace for that moment; the problem is that moment is fleeting and ultimately impossible to sustain and they can soon become your worst enemy.

Drugs, whether legally prescribed or illicit, hold a central position within the prison ecosystem, far outweighing the values promoted by the Scottish Prison System. They serve as the lifeblood of prison routines, surpassing any other form of currency behind those fortified walls. Whether involved in their distribution, consumption, smuggling, or possession, drugs dictate power dynamics within the prison community.

The allure of drugs lies in the unparalleled sense of control and security they offer. Within the confines of prison, power is a coveted commodity, as it grants safety and a measure of stability that is otherwise elusive. While similar dynamics can be observed outside prison walls, the intensity of drug influence within the prison system is unmatched. Drugs reign supreme, establishing themselves as the unrivaled sovereigns within those stark environments.

The underlying reason for this dominance is strikingly simple: drugs facilitate *'escapism'* and enable individuals to wield power. Those who have access to drugs hold power over their peers, attaining a position of authority that affords them a sense of luxury within the stark confines of prison life. When I say luxury, I mean a very limited amount of luxury; by no means can you ever have real luxury within prison. It is an unwritten truth that any prisoner who has endured a substantial sentence will tell you — drugs can transform an individual into a king within the prison walls, giving them power over the hall and access to all its **'limited'** luxuries. Alternatively, drugs offer an escape from the arduous realities of incarceration, providing solace and temporary respite from the daily hardships of prison existence.

While the allure of drugs is evident within prison walls, it is essential to recognise the detrimental effects they bring and the damage it does both mentally and physically to individuals who set off down this path. Substance abuse not only perpetuates the cycle of addiction but also exacerbates the challenges and dangers inherent to the prison environment. However, the undeniable power of drugs within prisons persists as they continue to shape the dynamics, aspirations, and, unfortunately, the fate of those confined behind bars.

Drugs can alter one's state of consciousness, providing a means to detach from the immediate surroundings and temporarily numb or distract from the emotional and mental strain of incarceration. The altered mental state induced by substance use can create a distorted sense of reality, blurring the harshness of the prison environment and momentarily transporting individuals away from their confinement, like a type of release for the day.

In the absence of healthier coping mechanisms or meaningful activities, drugs can become a readily available means to fill the void and alleviate the overwhelming sense of confinement. They offer a form of *'self-medication,'* providing a temporary sense of control and emotional relief. However, it's important to note that while drugs may provide an initial escape, they often heighten the underlying issues and challenges faced in prison.

Substance abuse not only inflicts severe harm on individuals but also exposes the vulnerable to greater risks within the prison environment. The progression into addiction amplifies the deterioration of physical and mental health, strains interpersonal connections, and heightens the likelihood of facing disciplinary actions or additional legal repercussions. Tragically, it is often the vulnerable addicts who bear the brunt of these consequences, perpetuating a cycle of despair and bitterness toward the system.

In prison, a disturbing pattern emerges where vulnerable individuals, already grappling with addiction, find themselves ensnared in further troubles. The dynamics of drug distribution within the prison environment are such that those involved in the trade rarely possess their own supply. Instead, they manipulate the vulnerable, utilising them as unwitting couriers or holders of whatever substance it may be. These vulnerable addicts, driven by desperation, become the unwitting carriers of additional prison sentences, exacerbating their already fragile mental states.

It is truly disheartening to witness the most vulnerable individuals trapped in the grip of addiction, becoming ensnared in the unforgiving cycle of the prison system. These individuals are driven by their insatiable cravings and deprived of the necessary support and fall victim to predatory behaviors by both prisoner and staff. Yet, it is important to recognise the complex interplay at play here.

On the other side of this dark coin, we encounter individuals who, having experienced trauma themselves, deploy self-preservation tactics to gain control over the drug-addicted prison population. They have developed a keen understanding of the prison dynamics, recognising that access to drugs, whether inside or outside prison, grants them power and influence. It is no coincidence that they often arrive with reputations that precede them, reflecting their propensity for seeking out power within the confines of the prison walls.

Their difficult upbringings and elevated scores on *'Adverse Childhood Experiences (ACEs)'* charts offer insight into the roots of their behaviors. It is important to recognise that their actions are a product of learned behaviors developed through a conditioning process that enables them to navigate the prison environment successfully, albeit at the expense of others. This approach allows these prisoners to carve out a relatively privileged existence within the confines of the prison walls. However, it is crucial to understand that this behavior leaves profound emotional scars on both the individuals perpetrating it and those affected by it.

The walls they construct to sustain this way of life become a defense mechanism, shielding them from the remorse and consequences of their actions. Nevertheless, the toll it takes on their psyche is profound, as they are forced to bury their humanity and suppress any empathy or remorse that may surface. The facade of success within the prison walls masks the deep emotional wounds and internal conflicts they carry, resulting from their chosen path.

While these individuals may appear to succeed temporarily within the prison environment, their actions perpetuate a cycle of harm and manipulation. They exploit the vulnerabilities of others, perpetuating a system of power dynamics that ultimately contribute to the overall deterioration of the prison community. The empathetic lens reveals the deeply rooted patterns and traumas that have shaped their behavior, yet it does not excuse the harm caused to others.

So what causes these *'sociopathic'* behaviors, sociopathic being a person with a personality disorder manifesting itself in extreme anti-social attitudes and behavior; prison being the perfect breeding ground for both prisoner and staff to learn these sociopathic tendencies? Many professionals point to **'ACES'** being a big part of why these learned behaviors manifest and ultimately end up in a hugely traumatised and conditioned prison population. So, what are **ACES**?

ACES stands for Adverse Childhood Experiences, which is a term used to describe a range of traumatic experiences that some individuals may have faced during their childhood. The original ACEs study conducted by the Centers for Disease Control and Prevention (CDC) and Kaiser Permanente identified the following categories of ACEs:

- Physical abuse: Experiencing physical harm or injury inflicted by a parent or caregiver.

- Sexual abuse: Involvement in sexual acts or activities without consent or understanding.

- Emotional abuse: Suffering from repeated emotional maltreatment, such as humiliation, belittlement, or constant criticism.

- Physical neglect: Lack of adequate supervision, shelter, or access to basic needs, resulting in physical harm or risk.

- Emotional neglect: Chronic disregard for a child's emotional well-being, such as ignoring their needs or emotional support.

- Household substance abuse: Growing up in a household where alcohol or drugs are abused leads to an unstable or unsafe environment.

- Household mental illness: Having a parent or caregiver with mental health issues, such as depression, anxiety, or severe mood swings.

- Parental separation or divorce: Witnessing the separation or divorce of parents or caregivers can lead to significant disruptions in family dynamics.

- Incarcerated household member: Having a family member, particularly a parent or caregiver, serving time in prison or jail.

- Domestic violence: Being exposed to violence between adult family members, such as witnessing physical altercations or hearing threats.

These adverse experiences can have long-lasting effects on an individual's physical, mental, and emotional well-being. The cumulative impact of multiple ACEs increases the risk of various health issues, including mental health disorders, substance abuse, and physical illnesses later in life.

In the 1990s, a pioneering study known as the Adverse Childhood Experiences (ACEs) study was conducted. It involved the recruitment of 17,000 adults who were asked about their experiences of childhood stressors and trauma, as well as their health outcomes.

This groundbreaking research sheds light on valuable insights regarding the treatment of substance abuse.

The ACE study demonstrates a significant correlation between adverse childhood experiences and an increased risk of developing substance abuse issues in adulthood. It reveals that individuals who have faced traumatic events during their early years are more susceptible to using substances as a coping mechanism or to numb emotional pain. This is amplified significantly in a prison setting. These adverse experiences, such as physical abuse, neglect, household dysfunction, or exposure to violence, can deeply impact an individual's psychological well-being and contribute to the development of substance abuse problems later in life.

The findings of the ACEs study highlight the importance of a trauma-informed approach in treating substance abuse. Recognising and addressing the underlying traumatic experiences that contribute to addiction is crucial for effective intervention and recovery. By acknowledging and understanding the connections between childhood trauma and substance abuse, healthcare providers and professionals can tailor treatment approaches that address both the addiction and the underlying trauma for each individual, however this practice seems to be non-existent in prison, no matter what their policies and legislation says.

That said, this agreement is more complex in a prison setting, and with a less than modest budget, it can seem at times fruitless to even bring up these complex factors, but for any healing to take place from a prisoner's perspective, the same understanding and empathetic methods must be applied; sadly this is not the case and for the most part is the opposite as the prison population feel no empathy for the staff, whilst the staff, mostly lacking in trauma-informed practice, have a punitive view towards the prisoners and also lack empathy for them; with some staff being very verbal about this, saying things like, "I would bring back hanging" or "if it was up to me, I would give you all bread and water." I have personally heard this multiple times from different staff members, but that being said, on the other hand, I have heard other staff voicing their opinions on this view by opposing what has been said and verbally challenging the view and suggesting that it is unhelpful to say things like that to prisoners. Whatever way you look at it, it's a conditioned minority of the population who live in a unique sub-community, which can, at times, cause radical and conditioned opinions.

Interventions informed by the ACEs study emphasise the need for holistic, comprehensive care that goes beyond mere substance use treatment. It involves incorporating trauma-focused therapies, counseling, and support systems that address the root causes of addiction and offending behaviours and promotes healing from past traumas. By integrating trauma-informed practices into substance abuse and offending treatment, individuals can have a better chance at long-term recovery, breaking the cycle of addiction and offending and achieving improved overall well-being.

Fritzi Hortsman created a project called *'The Compassionate Prison Project.'* This project was a project that aimed to bring compassion and understanding to the prison system. Their project focused on providing trauma-informed care and support to incarcerated individuals, recognising that many prisoners have experienced significant trauma throughout their lives.

Dr. Gabor Maté, a renowned physician and expert in addiction and trauma, and Fritzi Horstman, a filmmaker and advocate for criminal justice reform, collaborated to bring a project that showed the profound impact of childhood trauma on individuals who end up in the prison system, *'The Wisdom of Trauma'*, an amazing film, which sheds light on many of the underlying ACES, connected to the problems which haunt adult prisoners their whole entire lives and subconsciously fuels addiction and offending behaviour. They emphasize that understanding and addressing the underlying traumas, is essential for effective rehabilitation and reducing reoffending rates.

'The Compassionate Prison Project' promotes various initiatives, including educational programs, counseling services, and trauma-informed training for prison staff. They strive to create an environment that fosters healing, empathy, and personal growth for both incarcerated individuals and those working within the prison system.

By integrating trauma-informed care, the project seeks to break the cycle of trauma and addiction that often leads to repeated criminal behavior. It acknowledges that addressing the root causes of incarceration, such as childhood trauma, is essential for rehabilitation and reducing the likelihood of reoffending. They highlight the need for compassion and understanding and show how it can be a transformative force within the prison system.

By providing support, resources, and tools for personal growth, they showed how to create a more humane and effective approach to rehabilitation, ultimately working towards a more just and compassionate prison community. I had the pleasure of having Fritzi Hortsman as a guest on my podcast **'Social Sessions',** and let's just say if every prison had a Fritzi as governor, the prison population would be a much better and safer place to heal. Unfortunately, we need to be realistic and look at how our system operates, and an empathetic and compassionate approach is far from realistic most of the time.

Authenticity in chaos

"Dual Diagnosis" and **"ACES"** hold immense potential as key factors in healing our broken prison system. The current punitive model, devoid of training on trauma, ACES, or dual diagnosis, forces staff to navigate a treacherous landscape of mental health challenges, violence, and addiction. To survive, they must adapt to the harsh reality of prison life, becoming desensitised to violence, abuse, and trauma. This reality contributes to the high turnover rates among prison staff at Addiewell, with many leaving shortly after training and a huge amount of staff on sick pay due to mental health problems; this is due to the unnatural, unauthentic, and demanding nature of their work environment.

To effect meaningful change, prison staff must be trauma-informed, equipped to identify signs of PTSD or trauma onset, and educated on the root causes of addiction. It is crucial to understand that trauma and addiction cannot be punished out of a person. It requires a finely tuned process that involves time, empathy, compassion, and a heightened level of awareness that allows one to meet individuals at their own level. While these traits may be unique and challenging to cultivate, they are essential for instigating transformation within our prison system.

Merely recycling old methods under new names serves only to maintain a facade of adherence to standards. If we truly seek change, we must pride ourselves on creating a system that not only punishes individuals for their criminal acts but also endeavors to heal and rehabilitate them. Alternatively, we must honestly acknowledge that the prison system primarily functions as a holding unit until an individual's sentence is served and stop projecting a fake value system for the public and government and if subsequently the prison system makes our prisoners worse, then how can we blame them when they come out and reoffend?

In the pursuit of transformation, there is no denying the challenges that lie ahead. However, within these trials, we find hope in groundbreaking initiatives like **'SISCO and Phoenix's Recovery Cafes'** and the *'Compassionate Prison Project.'* By embracing empathy, compassion, and understanding, we can challenge the limitations of the current system and forge a path toward meaningful reform. Could it be time to change the cycle, embrace change, and establish a prison system that fosters true rehabilitation, healing, and a brighter future for all? I don't think our society is quite ready to empathise with our most vulnerable in society yet. I think the media do a great job in demonising drug addicts and traumatized prisoners, but there is hope, always hope, that one day we can have a prison system to be proud of rather than one that releases further traumatised and more **'unauthentic'** versions of individuals who went in.

As my time in Addiewell neared its conclusion, I realised that my experiences within the system had led me down a troubling path. Instead of finding my true self, I had learned to assimilate into the existing structure, losing touch with my **'authentic'** identity. Addiewell had provided me with insight into the hardships faced by countless prisoners and taught me, albeit badly learned, behaviours that had allowed me to survive and navigate through a very harsh terrain.

While some individuals found solace in learned behaviors that had served them well within the prison context, I believe this solace stems from a lack of self-awareness. At this point in my life, I was part of a system that I did not believe in or respect. I had managed to complete an honors bachelor of science degree, met my soul mate, and met some amazing people, both prisoner and staff, but as a whole, I was so far from my *'authentic'* self; I was in a place that many don't come back from. I had poor self-awareness and a bitter hatred towards a system that had wronged me so much and then left me to rot and fend for myself. The truth of the matter was I had been conditioned and become a statistic, doing the exact same things as 95% of the prison population.

During that period of my life, when I reached the age of thirty, I found myself in a fortunate position with an incredible partner by my side. To be honest, without her unwavering support, I doubt I would have been able to navigate the challenges I faced and emerge on the other side to share this tale. She stood by me and my family through thick and thin, accompanying us on a tumultuous rollercoaster ride of emotions encompassing helplessness, love, hate, resentment, and more. The range of feelings and the conditioning imposed by prison life made it difficult to keep pace and articulate, but I consider myself fortunate to have had a support network. Sadly, many others incarcerated with me lacked anything remotely resembling such a network. These individuals, in their quest to straddle the worlds inside and outside prison, find themselves assuming unauthentic personas, constantly adjusting their behaviors, manners, and morals. This tiresome process drains their spirit and creates a disconnection that is exceedingly arduous to repair.

Looking back, I now recognize that I was concealing a significant amount of fear and trauma, and to this day, I still am. In the absence of appropriate support, these learned behaviors became my default coping mechanisms, seemingly the only logical option available to navigate the challenging prison environment. Consequently, I chose not to delve deeply into the personal losses I endured, as they inflicted additional trauma that further fortified the emotional walls I had erected for self-protection. Regrettably, this only led me further away from my authentic self.

Understanding the complexities involved in finding solace within learned behaviors, I embark on a journey of self-awareness. While such behaviors may provide temporary relief from the hardships of prison life, they can hinder personal growth and impede true healing. It is through introspection and a heightened sense of self-awareness that I seek to unravel the layers of fear and trauma that have shaped my experiences.

As I progress on this path, I recognise the importance of creating a supportive environment conducive to self-awareness, healing, and personal growth. I endeavor to dismantle the emotional walls I have constructed, allowing vulnerability to guide me toward rediscovering my authentic self. This entails seeking the necessary help, guidance, and support to facilitate my journey of healing and self-discovery.

Chapter Eight: HMP Barlinnie – A Deceptive Mirage: The Top-End Illusion

As I embarked on my journey towards HMP Barlinnie's Letham Hall, a surge of hopefulness and reconnection coursed through my veins. A newfound thirst for personal growth had recently taken hold of me, fueled by the pages of self-help books like *"The Chimp Paradox"* and *"The Secret."* I yearned to reconnect with my authentic self, seeking solace in a more peaceful and nurturing environment. The prospect of this next chapter in my sentence filled me with hope and excitement.

Despite the unsettling tales that circulated among fellow prisoners about the notorious top end—stories of mistreatment, power-hungry staff, and unjust downgrades—I couldn't suppress a flicker of eagerness. Little did I know that some of those tales were, in fact, rooted in harsh reality.

The top end, a facet of the long sentence experience, held particular significance for those serving life sentences. The Top End is a part of your training for freedom process and is ultimately like a semi-open prison, where you get a lot more responsibility and freedom and it presented an invaluable opportunity to re-establish connections with loved ones and gradually reintegrate into pockets of society. I was fortunate to have a supportive personal officer who granted me the privilege of supervised escorted leaves (SEL) every six weeks. These visits allowed me to savor two precious hours with my family, and they served as a lifeline amidst the confines of prison life. Reliance officers vigilantly oversaw these visits, ensuring adherence to the rules was kept; unfortunately, life is life, and it depended on which reliance staff you got, which would lead to how much freedom you would get within the visit.

After my first year in Barlinnie, there was the promising opportunity of a work placement within the community. This program aimed to equip individuals with the skills necessary for future employment, reintroduce a sense of structure and routine, and foster a smoother reintegration into society.

The mere prospect of supervised visits and the chance to engage in meaningful work kindled a profound sense of hope within me. It was a glimmer of normalcy, a vital step towards reclaiming a sense of purpose and rediscovering my authentic self. Little did I realize the trials and transformative experiences that awaited me on this poignant journey of reconnecting with my family, rebuilding my life, and taking one deliberate step at a time; unfortunately, this ended up feeling like you were taking two back some of the time.

As I arrived at HMP Barlinnie, the disparity between this prison and HMP Addiewell became immediately apparent. Barlinnie was a staff-run facility, and the staff made it abundantly clear that this was their domain. If you sought a well-organized holding prison solely focused on enforcing court-ordered sentences, Barlinnie was the epitome of such an establishment. There was no room for ambiguity; the prevailing sentiment within those walls was the unwavering acknowledgment that you were firmly entrenched in the grip of imprisonment.

HMP Barlinnie, the largest and arguably the toughest Scottish prison, carried its formidable reputation with an air of infamy. The biggest distributor of methadone and its notoriously violent culture and its segregation unit known as the Wendy House all set Barlinnie alone in its own mythical sense of notoriety. However, nestled within this imposing institution, the top-end conditions provided glimpses of positivity and a departure from the conventional prison experience. It created a distinct microcosm, akin to a prison within a prison, where a different atmosphere permeated the air.

Within the top-end, we enjoyed a degree of freedom not typically found in the confines of Barlinnie. We resided in a separate hall (Letham Hall), shielded from the rigors of the main prison. This afforded us the luxury of more time spent outside in the yard, the ability to come and go with greater flexibility, and expanded opportunities to engage in physical activities. The gym became a sanctuary, and when the staff found the motivation, we savored extra football games.

Contrary to popular belief, the top-end in Barlinnie possessed positive elements. It wasn't solely a realm of hardships and restrictions. The allure of home visits and the prospect of a work placement served as powerful incentives for us to exhibit good behavior and strive to reconnect with our true selves. These opportunities kindled a sense of hope, propelling us forward on a path of personal growth and reintegration.

Despite the overarching challenges of prison life, the top end at Barlinnie offered a glimmer of respite and encouragement. It provided a space where we could embrace fleeting moments of freedom, engage in physical activities, and actively work towards re-establishing our authentic identities. Amidst the struggles, we clung to these silver linings as beacons of motivation and reminders that positive change was within our grasp.

Beyond the Facade: Exposing the Realities of the Top-End:

Top-end conditions undeniably hold immense potential, presenting a concept that, if executed with the right structure and attitude, could truly transform individuals who have endured turbulent years within violent and aggressive prisons. There is no prison idea that will ever help every prisoner. The sad fact of the matter is that our society outside of prison walls is built in such a way that crime will always be there. The idea behind the top-end offers a glimmer of hope—a chance for individuals to transition into a more positive and supportive environment.

The underlying notion of the top-end is to shift away from the prevailing *"us versus them"* mentality that often plagues prison facilities. It seeks to create an atmosphere where the lines between staff and prisoners become less pronounced, fostering a sense of unity and mutual respect. In an ideal scenario, the top end could serve as a catalyst for transformative change, promoting rehabilitation, personal growth, and a genuine reintegration into society.

The truth of the matter is that we find a power dynamic where the prisoner has very little power, and the officer has a lot. This means that if a relationship is formed where a prisoner and a staff member do not like each other, the prison officer can make life very hard for him, much more than in mainstream conditions. This, unfortunately, makes prisoners build more walls to protect them from the potential dangers they see, causing more anxiety and paranoia, which in turn creates another vortex to be filled, and in prison, there is nothing like more drugs to fill that vortex.

The top end reminded me of the 'Stanford Prison Experiment', which we already spoke about. The experiment aimed to investigate the psychological effects of perceived power and authority in the context of a simulated prison environment. Volunteers were randomly assigned roles as either prisoners or guards and were placed in a simulated prison setting for a short duration. The study had to be prematurely terminated due to the extreme and unethical behavior displayed by some of the participants, highlighting the profound influence of situational factors on human behavior.

The Stanford Prison Experiment, conducted by psychologist Philip Zimbardo in 1971, remains a landmark study in understanding the profound impact of environments on human behavior and the erosion of authenticity. While it may not directly relate to the top-end conditions at Barlinnie, there are parallels that can be drawn in terms of the influence of the environment on individual authenticity.

The study highlighted how the environment, in this case, a simulated prison, has the capacity to override individuals' inherent authenticity. As the participants adapted to the power dynamics and expectations of their roles, their behavior became increasingly divorced from their true selves. The guards, who were not inherently sadistic, took on authoritarian personas, while the prisoners, who were not inherently submissive, internalized their roles of subjugation.

Similarly, in the context of the top-end conditions at Barlinnie, the prison environment can exert a powerful influence on individuals' authenticity. The coercive and restrictive nature of incarceration, combined with the dynamics between staff and prisoners, can lead individuals to adopt behaviors and personas that are incongruent with their true selves.

Within the top end, where there may be greater freedoms and opportunities for connection with the outside world, individuals may still feel the weight of the prison system and its expectations. The need to navigate complex power dynamics, adhere to rules and regulations, and protect oneself can create a disconnection from one's authentic self. The pressure to conform to the demands and norms of the prison environment can erode individuality, leading to a fragmented sense of identity.

Ultimately, understanding the influence of the environment on authenticity underscores the importance of creating supportive and empowering spaces within any prison system. By fostering environments that encourage self-expression, personal growth, and genuine rehabilitation, individuals can have a better opportunity to retain and rediscover their authentic selves, even in the face of challenging circumstances.

However, it is important to acknowledge that reality often falls short of this lofty vision. Instead of bridging the divide, the **"us versus them"** mentality sometimes becomes more pronounced within the top-end. Existing tensions and power dynamics can be magnified, further exacerbating the challenges faced by both staff and prisoners.

Power dynamics taint authenticity, particularly when it comes to individuals in positions of authority, such as prison officers. The wielding of power can create a sense of superiority and entitlement that can lead to a disconnection from one's authentic self. In an environment like Barlinnie, especially the top end, where power imbalances are prevalent, it becomes even more critical to examine how these dynamics impact authenticity.

Social norms and preconceived notions about prisoners can significantly influence an officer's way of working. Society often stigmatises and dehumanises individuals who are incarcerated, leading to biases and negative perceptions. These biases can seep into the mindset of prison officers, shaping their attitudes and interactions with prisoners.

In an environment like Barlinnie, where staff are conditioned to view prisoners with suspicion and maintain a certain level of distance, any officer who tries to genuinely help or connect with prisoners may be seen as the **"odd one out."** This can create a sense of isolation and ostracism for those officers who genuinely want to make a positive difference.

The culture within Barlinnie, where both staff and prisoners may exhibit behaviors akin to a gang mentality, further complicates the situation. The staff may feel pressure to conform to the established norms and expectations of their colleagues, perpetuating an **"us versus them"** mentality that permeates the prison environment. This group mentality can reinforce existing biases and hinder the development of authentic, empathetic relationships between staff and prisoners.

As I reflect on a particular incident in HMP Barlinnie, a vivid memory resurfaces, revealing the conditioning that permeates both sides of the prison environment. I witnessed a woman choking during a visitation, clearly in distress and in need of immediate assistance. Astonishingly, the staff remained motionless, seemingly oblivious or perhaps desensitised to the situation. The assumption that she was choking on drugs may have influenced their inaction, perpetuating the notion of *"leave her be."*

As the woman's partner shouted desperately for help, I scanned the room, witnessing the apathy that engulfed the visitors. At that critical moment, I felt an undeniable urge to act. Without hesitation, I rushed to the woman's aid, driven solely by the instinct to save a life. My sole focus was on helping her, without any regard for the potential repercussions or indirect implications for the officers.

After successfully assisting her and dislodging the object causing the choking, the officers sprang into action, inspecting the substance she had expelled. It was at this moment that a chilling realisation dawned upon me—what if it had been drugs she had projected? In inadvertently saving her life, I could have unwittingly aided the officers in catching her passing drugs. The fear of this realisation shook me to my core, and I vowed silently never to react in a similar manner again.

This mentality, shaped by the prison environment, is unquestionably unhealthy for all involved. The lack of immediate assistance demonstrated by both staff and visitors exemplifies the conditioning at play. It highlights the desensitisation and disregard for the well-being of individuals, fueled by the pervasive belief that offering aid could indirectly assist law enforcement efforts.

Upon returning to the hall, one of the officers extended his hand, commending me for saving the woman's life. However, I refused to shake his hand, feeling conflicted and resentful. This act further strained the already fragile relationship between us. It saddened me deeply to realise the extent to which we are conditioned. Even within the supposedly more supportive confines of a top-end facility, someone nearly choking to death still is not enough to overcome the generations of conditioning at play.

The incident serves as a stark reminder of the pervasive conditioning on both sides of the prison walls. It reveals the deeply ingrained patterns of behavior and thinking that undermine the genuine humanity and empathy that should prevail in such environments. It highlights the urgent need to challenge and transform this conditioning, fostering a culture that prioritizes compassion, support, and the well-being of all individuals involved. However, we are so far from this culture, and if and when we do start to try and change things, it will be a long, slow, drawing-out process.

For staff in prison to maintain their authenticity within such an environment requires immense self-awareness, empathy, and a commitment to treating individuals with dignity and respect. It requires challenging and questioning the prevailing norms and behaviors, even if it means standing apart from the collective mindset. By recognising the humanity of prisoners, valuing their potential for growth and change, and embracing a restorative approach, officers can strive to foster a more authentic and compassionate environment within the prison system.

In order to address the issue effectively, it is crucial for prison management to promote a culture that supports and encourages authenticity, empathy, and professionalism among staff. This can involve implementing training programs that focus on fostering positive relationships, addressing biases, and nurturing a rehabilitative mindset. Additionally, creating spaces for open dialogue and feedback can help challenge existing norms and encourage staff to reflect on their attitudes and behaviors.

Authenticity in chaos

In 2022, I attended a meeting at HMP Lowmoss where I put forth a suggestion: the implementation of a course that would bring together both staff and prisoners. The goal would be to foster a space where we could openly share our experiences of traumatic events, listen to one another, and work towards building trust and understanding. The intention was to confront our inherent biases, desensitised mentalities, and the disconnection from our own authenticity. I believe that through this process, we could bridge the gaps and develop a greater awareness of each other's true selves.

Sadly, I never received any response from the prison, leaving me with the impression that they were not ready to undertake the challenging task of bridging these divides. This lack of response only reinforces the existing division and erodes any sense of trust between staff and prisoners. The idea of such a course may appear radical within the prison system, and it would undoubtedly face significant resistance from both sides. However, it is only through understanding, acceptance, and genuine connection that healing can occur. By seeing one another in our true forms and raising our awareness, we can begin to break down barriers and build a foundation of empathy and mutual respect.

Acknowledging the impact of power dynamics, social norms, and ingrained thoughts about prisoners is crucial in creating an environment that values authenticity, empathy, and fairness for both staff and prisoners. However, for this transformation to take place, there must be a genuine willingness to change within the prison system. It requires a collective effort to challenge the status quo, confront biases, and actively work towards fostering a culture of understanding and growth. The reality is, prison is not a vote winner and understandably not, especially in the current cost of living crisis. That said, if we want our prison system to change positively, we must sell it and explain with mindfulness, courage and intention that in the long run this will save a lot of money for the taxpayer and also make society a safer place.

While the road may be difficult and met with resistance, attempting to bridge these gaps is not only logical but **'essential'** for the healing of the prison system. By embracing the radical idea of bringing staff and prisoners together in a meaningful way, we can initiate a transformative process that offers the potential for a more compassionate, empathetic, and ultimately rehabilitative environment. It is through these efforts that we can begin to mend the deep wounds and divisions that currently plague the prison system, paving the way for a brighter and more inclusive future.

The role of the media in fostering a positive and impactful relationship between staff and prisoners cannot be underestimated. The impact of media on efforts to bridge gaps and transform the prison system extends beyond its influence on public perception. It also significantly affects the staff members working within the prison environment. The negative portrayal of prisoners and sensationalized stories perpetuated by the media can have detrimental effects on the attitudes and well-being of those working within the prison system.

Constant exposure to negative media narratives can contribute to the development or reinforcement of biases and prejudices held by staff members. The media's focus on extreme cases and incidents of misconduct can create an atmosphere of heightened suspicion and distrust towards prisoners. This, in turn, can contribute to a negative and adversarial dynamic between staff and prisoners, impeding the potential for meaningful rehabilitation and positive interactions.

Furthermore, media representations that emphasise the punitive aspects of prison life may lead to a sense of disillusionment among staff members. When faced with an overwhelming narrative that

109

emphasises punishment and dehumanisation, it can be challenging for staff to envision their role as facilitators of rehabilitation and agents of positive change. The constant exposure to negative media portrayals may erode their motivation, dampen their sense of empathy, and contribute to burnout or cynicism.

It is crucial to recognize the importance of providing staff members with accurate, balanced, and nuanced information about the prison system. By offering insights into successful rehabilitation programs, showcasing stories of transformation, and highlighting the positive aspects of their work, the media can play a significant role in shaping a more positive and supportive environment for staff members. This can contribute to fostering a sense of purpose, promoting job satisfaction, and encouraging staff to view their role as integral to the rehabilitation process.

In addition, promoting media literacy and critical thinking among staff members can empower them to question and challenge the narratives presented by the media. By encouraging them to seek out diverse perspectives and engage in discussions that challenge stereotypes, staff members can develop a more nuanced understanding of the complexities within the prison system.

Ultimately, it is essential to acknowledge the influence of media on staff members and work towards mitigating its negative effects. By providing accurate and balanced representations, promoting media literacy, and fostering an environment that values rehabilitation and compassion, we can support the well-being and professional growth of staff members while advancing the transformative goals of the prison system and essentially make prison, at the very least, an environment that as a society we can proud of attempting to achieve a level of rehabilitation.

During my time at HMP Barlinnie from 2016 to 2018, spending just over two years in the top end before transferring to HMP Castle Huntly, I witnessed the damaging effects of trauma on individuals. The rate of downgrades and unsuccessful transitions from top-end conditions was dishearteningly high. Unfortunately, obtaining accurate statistics on the success rates is challenging, as the prison system often avoids disclosing the embarrassing numbers of individuals sent back to closed, mainstream conditions.

If I were to estimate, I would say that perhaps only around twenty percent of those who went through top-end conditions were able to progress to the open estate, such as HMP Castle Huntly, and even that estimation may be generous. I personally witnessed individuals making repeated attempts—up to ten times—in the hopes of successfully navigating top-end conditions, only to face failure each time, with drug-related issues being a prevailing factor. It became all too common for individuals to experience multiple failures before finally reaching the open estate, where an entirely new set of challenges awaited them.

The significant number of individuals who struggle to succeed in top-end conditions can be attributed to the deep-rooted trauma they carry as a result of their experiences within the prison environment. The complete disconnection from one's authentic self and the ongoing exposure to the harsh realities of prison life inflict profound emotional and psychological wounds. These traumas manifest in various ways, often leading to struggles with substance abuse, which further complicate their journey towards successful rehabilitation.

The prison system, as it stands, falls short of adequately addressing and healing these underlying traumas. The lack of comprehensive trauma-informed care, even as prisoners try to reintegrate back into society, perpetuates a cycle of repeated failures and setbacks for individuals attempting to transition from top-end conditions to the open estate. It highlights the urgent need for a more holistic approach that recognises and addresses the profound impact of trauma on incarcerated individuals.

The lottery of who is governor in a certain prison when you move on through the system is also a factor that must be looked at critically. For example you may be lucky enough to arrive in HMP Barlinnie when Mick Stoney is governor, a governor who I personally respect as a fair and progressive thinking governor or you could end up with Brian Ironside, whom I believe has outdated thoughts on punishment and how prisoners should be treated; again everyone will have a differing opinion on this, but for it to be an influential reason on how you may be treated, seen or even how your sentence is managed, I do not think is a fair process.

Brian Ironside once told a group of us in HMP Barlinnie he was stopping supervised escorted leave, because he didn't think we needed it. Furthermore he went on whilst being questioned to say that because our families had not stopped us committing crimes in the first place, what good would these visits be for us? To put this in perspective there are only two top end prisons, one in Barlinnie and the other in Greenock, these visits would still be taking place in Greenock and if you read into training for freedom, rebuilding connections with families is a huge part of the process. This example just highlights the contradictions between prisons and different prison officials. The power prison officials are delegated is enormous and the lottery can be very confusing and debilitating for structural life as an individual living in these conditions.

Reforming the system requires a concerted effort to provide trauma-informed interventions, therapeutic support, and comprehensive rehabilitation programs that go beyond punitive measures. By acknowledging and actively working to heal the deep-seated traumas experienced by individuals within the prison environment, we can begin to break the cycle of repeated failures and offer a genuine pathway towards successful reintegration into society, but as it stands, Scotland is not quite ready for this kind of huge, radical change that the system needs, and this is played out in societal views on prisoners and the media's view of what prison actually is. These are some recent media headlines:

- **Fury as hundreds of prisoners get to vote in Scottish council elections because of SNP's 'soft touch justice' – Tom Martin, Scottish Daily Express**
- **Killers and other life prisoners released despite posing 'danger to the public' under soft-touch SNP – Richard Percival, Scottish Daily Express.**
- **Scottish prisoners could be freed after serving a third of the sentence.**
- **SNP calls for a more flexible system that allows earlier release with tagging, but Holyrood Tories criticize 'reckless, soft-touch' proposals**

"Constant soft touch media coverage can be detrimental to the progression and reform efforts within prisons for a number of reasons."

Excessive negative or lenient media portrayals of prisons can create a false sense of security and accomplishment. When media coverage emphasises only the success stories of *'hard justice'* and downplays the challenges and underlying issues within the prison system, it can lead to complacency and a lack of urgency for necessary reforms. This can hinder the motivation to address systemic problems and implement meaningful changes that truly promote rehabilitation and reduce reoffending rates.

Authenticity in chaos

Secondly, an overly positive media narrative can contribute to a public perception that the prison system is already functioning well and effectively rehabilitating individuals. This can result in reduced public pressure and advocacy for comprehensive reforms, as there may be a misguided belief that the current state of prisons is satisfactory. The lack of critical scrutiny and accountability in media coverage can impede the necessary societal engagement and demand for systemic improvements.

Additionally, constant soft-touch media coverage may overshadow the stories and experiences of those who have been negatively affected by the prison system. It can silence the voices of individuals who have experienced mistreatment, lack of access to education and mental health support, or inadequate reintegration opportunities; basic human rights breaches which consistently go on and please do not let anyone tell you any different. Some people may be of the opinion that prisoners should not have human rights and I get and hear this argument but that is not what is legislated and not what is promoted, so as far as this goes the system is in constant breach of human rights, **'daily'**, no matter what your opinion is on the matter. By not highlighting these important aspects, the media perpetuates a one-sided narrative that fails to address the full range of challenges and necessary changes within the prison system.

Moreover, an unbalanced and overly positive media portrayal can undermine public trust in the accuracy and credibility of media reporting. When individuals perceive a lack of critical analysis and an overreliance on superficial or sensationalised narratives, they may dismiss media coverage as biased or unreliable. This can lead to a diminished impact of media messaging and reduce the potential for meaningful public discourse and engagement on prison reform.

To ensure genuine progress and meaningful change within prisons, media coverage should strike a balance between highlighting positive developments and critically examining the existing challenges. By presenting a comprehensive and accurate depiction of the prison system, media can help foster informed public discussions, encourage necessary reforms, and ultimately contribute to the creation of more effective, humane, and rehabilitative prison systems.

Magazines like the Digger in Scotland epitomize the dangers of sensationalizing crime. Rather than promoting responsible journalism, this publication thrives on nonsensical gossip that often distorts the truth. The stories within the Digger serve no purpose other than to sensationalise crime and perpetuate a distorted image of *'gangsterism'* in Scotland. Sadly, this pursuit of sensationalism comes at the expense of ethical reporting and the potential to exacerbate already existing violent conflicts.

By exploiting serious issues such as poverty and drug problems for monetary profit, publications like The Digger fail to address the underlying causes and complexities of these societal challenges. Sensationalising crime may attract attention and boost sales, but it does little to contribute to a deeper understanding or offer meaningful solutions. Instead, it perpetuates a cycle of misinformation, stigmatisation, and sensationalism that hampers genuine progress.

Furthermore, this focus on sensationalised crime stories often overlooks the systemic factors that contribute to criminal behavior i.e. poverty, social inequality, and lack of access to education and resources, which all play significant roles in the perpetuation of crime. Reducing complex issues to sensationalised headlines and gossip-driven narratives, these publications divert attention from the root causes and hinder efforts to address them effectively.

Moreover, the glorification of *'gangsterism'* and the validation of violent conflicts through sensationalised reporting can have far-reaching consequences. It perpetuates a culture of violence and feeds into existing feuds, escalating tensions and putting lives at risk. By sensationalising these conflicts for profit, publications like the Digger are complicit in perpetuating a dangerous cycle of violence rather than contributing to constructive dialogue or solutions.

To address these issues responsibly, it is crucial for media outlets to prioritise ethical journalism and responsible reporting. Sensationalism should be replaced with thoughtful analysis, research-based reporting, and a commitment to understanding the underlying social issues that contribute to crime. By highlighting the systemic factors and advocating for meaningful change, the media can play a critical role in promoting a more informed and compassionate approach to addressing crime and its root causes in society.

The Recovery Café within HMP Barlinnie:

During my time serving my sentence, I was approached in 2016 with an opportunity to contribute to a project aimed at introducing a recovery café model into the prison system. However, the journey to implement this change was fraught with enormous barriers and resistance from prison security and hierarchy. Natalie and Danny, the individuals with whom I first discussed the café idea, fought tirelessly to create something meaningful within HMP Barlinnie. The café became a safe space for people to discuss their problems, predominantly related to drug issues, but we also made efforts to accommodate those with mental health concerns, providing a confidential environment for them to address any prison-related challenges.

The café was groundbreaking in its concept, but we faced numerous challenges. We had to fight for a separate room without staff presence, as it was widely accepted that prisoners would not feel comfortable being open and truthful if staff members were present, *again showing the 'us and them' mentality*. In collaboration with a dedicated officer, whom I have chosen not to name for anonymity, we presented the café project at the College of the Scottish Prison System in Polmont. We addressed an audience comprising prison managers, governors, addiction nurses, heads of healthcare, and drug forum leaders. They all recognised the need for more radical changes, such as the café, within the prison system.

However, the reality is that promoting a governor with liberal ideas and advocating for a human rights approach toward prisoners is often met with resistance. The fear of being labeled as an "easy touch" on crime prevents politicians from embracing a manifesto that includes investment in prisons and prisoners. This reluctance underscores the need for broader societal change before we can effectively address these issues. Until we stop deceiving ourselves about the significant and invaluable changes occurring within prisons, progress will remain elusive.

I can personally attest that during my entire time in prison from 2005 to 2015, there was no substantial change. It is disingenuous and insulting for the Scottish Prison Service to suggest otherwise. Our prison system is crumbling under immense pressure from a strict and challenging budget, while the majority of society continues to view prisoners as undeserving of support or inclusion. Admittedly, this perspective is reinforced when we predominantly focus on the extreme end of the crime spectrum.

Authenticity in chaos

To truly reform the prison system, we must confront these harsh realities and work towards transforming societal attitudes and perceptions. It requires a concerted effort to challenge stereotypes, prioritise rehabilitation, and advocate for a more compassionate and effective approach to prisoners. Only then can we begin to address the deep-rooted issues within our prisons and work toward meaningful change that benefits individuals, communities, and society as a whole.

The recovery café, an oasis of hope within the walls of HMP Barlinnie, stood as a shining beacon of progress in an otherwise bleak system. Its success was undeniable, prompting its expansion to various prisons throughout Scotland. However, resistance to such transformative initiatives remained, epitomized by governors like that of HMP Edinburgh, who stubbornly refused to embrace the concept due to a recovery café not being able to function without the presence of staff members. I do not know the governor of HMP Edinburgh, and he will have his reasons, but surely acting like this, ends up with some prisoners getting more help than others, does not make sense. An example of why this does not make sense can be seen here:

Allow me to illustrate the tragic consequences of this resistance through the heartbreaking story of Peter. Serving a daunting 10-year sentence, Peter found solace and support in the recovery café during his time in top-end conditions at HMP Barlinnie. The positive impact was evident as he made significant strides, giving up street valium (etizolam) and steadily reducing his methadone intake to just 30ml per day. Openly sharing his desire to wean himself off methadone, he voiced his fears of succumbing to the allure of etizolam once more, openly and candidly in a safe place, without judgment or the impulse to be dishonest, and this open support kept Peter away from etizolam.

Tragedy struck when Peter received the devastating news of his nephew's untimely death. Overwhelmed with grief, he turned to the recovery café for solace, only to find that he had been transferred back to HMP Edinburgh as they had drug tested him the day after his nephew died, knowing that Peter had used drugs in the past as a crutch during hard times. So when Peter eventually came around from his relapse, he had been moved to a prison without a recovery café.

In a cruel twist of fate, after the discovery that there was no recovery café within this establishment—a cruel void where his lifeline once existed. Without the support and guidance he so desperately needed, Peter, overcome by despair, relapsed on the potent and dangerous etizolam that circulated within the prison walls.

The consequences were dire. Unaccustomed to the potency of the drug that now coursed through his veins, Peter succumbed to its deadly grip, and his life was tragically cut short. The absence of a recovery café, a crucial lifeline that could have offered him the necessary support during his darkest moments, played a pivotal role in this devastating outcome.

This poignant tale serves as a powerful reminder of the profound significance behind initiatives like the recovery café within the prison system. In the past, the mere thought of providing prisoners with a space of their own, devoid of constant supervision, would have been unimaginable within the confines of HMP Barlinnie. However, times are changing, and the emergence of the recovery café movement has brought forth remarkable progress.

Witnessing the transformative impact of these cafes has been nothing short of inspiring. They have acted as lifelines for countless individuals, offering much-needed support and solace. However, the soaring demand for these spaces reveals the pressing need for expanded resources and an increased focus on addressing the complex needs and issues that prisoners have grown accustomed to over time. The waiting lists, unfortunately, remain long, leaving limited time to fully delve into the crucial work required for true rehabilitation.

Yet, it is these very initiatives that hold the key to reshaping the prison system and fostering a culture of compassion and empathy. By providing spaces where prisoners are treated as humans deserving of dignity, understanding, and support, we create an environment that is conducive to lasting change. When individuals are met with kindness and genuine care, their potential for transformation becomes evident.

Let us not forget the profound wisdom encapsulated in words, *"If you treat a person like an animal, don't be surprised when they exhibit animalistic behavior."* This quote serves as a poignant reminder that the way we treat others directly influences their responses and behaviors. By recognizing the humanity within each individual, irrespective of their past mistakes, we can cultivate an environment that encourages growth, rehabilitation, and, ultimately, the possibility of a brighter future.

Within the confines of Addiewell prison, the dedicated workers of the recovery cafe faced an immense challenge. They were allotted a mere two hours per week to address the intricate and multi-faceted issues burdening the incarcerated individuals. It was a fleeting window of opportunity, but within those limited hours, a lifeline emerged in the form of the recovery cafe. Operated by a charitable organization, this oasis provided solace, support, and a space for prisoners to connect and heal.

It was a brief respite where prisoners could speak openly about their addictions mental health issues, and rediscover their true selves.

However, the constraints of time made it a constant struggle to provide the comprehensive support needed. The dedicated recovery team at HMP Addiewell, driven by a commitment to change, remains hopeful and resilient in their efforts to improve the lives of prisoners.

Despite its undeniable impact, the café's potential has remained stifled by its confined operating hours. The prison, facing constant financial strains and resource limitations, struggled to provide adequate support for the initiative. The café, run by compassionate volunteers and compassionate prison staff, relied solely on their unwavering dedication and the goodwill of the charitable organization to operate without burdening the prison's already strained budget. The truth is concepts like the café are still met with disdain by many of the conditioned staff who see the café as a waste of time on a population of people who will never change.

They can be aggravated by the support they get, whilst the staff also come up short on support. As I have said before, the prison environment is a beast like no other, and it traumatises the vast majority of people within the blizzard of negativity and destruction. There is no doubt that staff should have the same support as prisoners as they see the same, live the same, and become conditioned the same. The reality of prison life is harsh, and this can lead to a he gets, she gets mentality, which is completely understandable but totally counter-productive when searching for true 'authenticity' and the kind of 'healing' needed in this specific environment.

The complex issues prisoners faced required more time, attention, and resources to address effectively. From grappling with addiction and mental health challenges to the new push by the Scottish Government, who believe prisoners should be taught their basic human rights to empower themselves and learn the legal complexities of human rights along with MAT standards (Medical Assistance Treatment Standards). This huge push and we don't even have a true piece of legislation to work on yet; due to *'Brexit'* no one knows what the Bill of Rights will be or what it will contain.

Through the Recovery café in HMP Barlinnie, we were introduced to Ged and Derek from Reach Advocacy, a very well-organized agency, that almost seven years ago tried to do the same thing in HMP Barlinnie by trying to empower the prisoners with human rights and knowledge of the MAT standards. They tried their hardest, but for whatever reason, we were told one week that they would not be coming back. As prisoners, we made jokes about the fact that too many prisoners were going to their doctors and telling prison officers their rights, but in all honesty, this was probably true, and to see them now push a full agenda nearly a decade later is embarrassing and so disingenuous as, they know that this will make very little difference.

I can assure you the last thing the SPS wants is a bunch of prisoners who know their rights and know what MAT standards are, writing off to their lawyers and local MSPs. The prison would have a dozen lawsuits out against it within a month if this was properly imposed on the system. If anything, there will be a watered-down version written into the prison rules and legislation somewhere, and please believe me, the last thing on a prisoner's mind is a prison rule were they know they are entitled to nothing within it. The ability to converse with a prison doctor about the best course of action for me is very radical, in my opinion. I do hope I am wrong, but I cannot see this making any change to how day-to-day prison life plays out.

These are prison concepts that are so radical that they will never even get off the ground, in my opinion. I am often told I think too big and often overlook the smaller progress in prison. However, I do see the smaller progress, "I think", but by the time they are implemented, there are another two that have arisen. I am not unaware that I will be biased from time to time from an ex-prisoner's point of view, but I don't believe I am that biased to see recycled materials and concepts that plague the prison's chances of becoming a better place to become 'authentic.' To try and empower each prisoner with human rights and an efficient knowledge of MAT standards, in my opinion, is only giving the prisoner false hopes that I have seen dashed over and over again, only making things worse and giving you a way of thinking that is very hard to regress from: *"whatever happens, happens and anything else is a bonus."*

This mindset is a horrible mindset, and living with it long enough can have catastrophic effects on confidence, self-esteem, belief, self-worth, self-identity, purpose, and many more damaging effects; I know this because I have lived it and I have also seen many people liberated with that mindset which has ultimately led to the sum we spoke of earlier mental health = addiction = dual diagnosis; **'now you are in trouble'**. Being liberated with this mindset is toxic and dangerous, and it's a well-established mindset found within the Scottish Prison System.

Renowned professionals like Jordan Peterson, Gabor Mate, and Joe Dispenza have shed light on the fascinating concept of brain plasticity, which refers to the brain's ability to change and adapt throughout our lives. They explain that our brains are wired to seek the path of least resistance in order to satisfy our desires. However, these experts suggest that it is possible to rewire our brains, a process that they claim can take as little as 28 days.

The question then arises: How is such brain rewiring achievable within the current conditions of prisons? This is a valid concern, as the lasting effects of long-term incarceration on individuals, including myself, have been witnessed first-hand. The prison environment, with its inherent challenges and limitations, poses significant obstacles to promoting brain rewiring and facilitating positive change.

In order for brain rewiring to occur, it requires a nurturing environment that fosters growth, empathy, and personal development. Unfortunately, many prisons struggle to provide such an environment due to various factors, including overcrowding, limited resources, prison undercurrent, violence, drugs, and a predominant focus on punishment rather than rehabilitation.

Nonetheless, it is crucial to acknowledge that the potential for change exists, even within these challenging circumstances. Although the current prison system may not adequately facilitate brain rewiring, efforts can still be made to create spaces and programs that encourage personal growth and transformation. Implementing innovative approaches, such as therapy, education, vocational training, and supportive rehabilitation programs, can play a pivotal role in empowering individuals to rewire their brains and rebuild their lives.

While it is true that the road to rewiring the brain within prison conditions is fraught with obstacles, it is not an insurmountable task. By acknowledging the need for systemic change, advocating for compassionate and evidence-based approaches to rehabilitation, and investing in resources and support systems, we can create an environment that nurtures brain rewiring and enables individuals to have the best opportunity possible.

The journey to change is seldom easy, but by embracing compassion, empathy, and a commitment to rehabilitation, prisons can become spaces that promote healing, growth, and genuine transformation. Let us strive for a system that allocates the time, resources, and support necessary to give every individual the opportunity to rebuild their lives and forge a better future. This would seem to me to be a better approach than offering knowledge of legislation and rights that very few prisoners will have the awareness to navigate.

To transform this scenario, a simple solution lay within the recovery cafe. By allocating additional time and resources to the café, the prison could expand its operating hours and enhance the support services provided. With extended hours, more prisoners could access the café, fostering a sense of community and offering a platform for empowerment and healing.

Moreover, forging partnerships with external organizations, legal experts, and healthcare professionals could amplify the impact of the café's services. By leveraging these collaborations, the prison could provide prisoners with a comprehensive understanding of their human rights, offer specialized treatment options, and facilitate their reintegration into society. A safe place is needed for these new and radical changes that the Scottish Recovery Consortium would like to become foundational within the SPS. Let me ask you a simple question: do you think giving prisoners knowledge of their human rights and showing them MAT standards will make any difference in the prison system I have described to you? Do you think society is ready for prisoners to have human rights and to be able to express them in a prison setting?

While some individuals question the feasibility of granting prisoners full human rights in prison, others argue passionately for the dignity and inherent worth of every individual, including prisoners. They believe that denying basic human rights can perpetuate cycles of violence and dehumanisation, further alienating individuals from society.

The debate surrounding prisoners' human rights is complex. It requires careful consideration of balancing security and control with the promotion of rehabilitation and reintegration. Recognizing and respecting the human rights of prisoners can contribute to creating an environment that fosters rehabilitation, reduces reoffending rates, and ultimately leads to a safer and more just society.

Engaging in an open dialogue and exploring best practices from around the world can help inform the development of a more humane and equitable prison system. It requires a nuanced understanding, a willingness to challenge existing beliefs and biases, and a commitment to creating an environment that respects the fundamental rights of all individuals, regardless of their circumstances.

Scandinavia is often cited as an example of a region where prisoners' human rights and rehabilitation are prioritised within the prison system. Countries like Norway, Sweden, and Denmark have embraced a more progressive approach to incarceration, focusing on the principles of rehabilitation, dignity, and respect.

In Scandinavian prisons, the emphasis is placed on creating environments that promote personal growth, education, vocational training, and mental health support. Prisoners are treated with dignity and are provided with opportunities to develop skills that can help them reintegrate into society upon release. These countries have recognized the importance of addressing the underlying issues that contribute to criminal behavior, such as addiction, poverty, mental health struggles, and lack of education or employment prospects.

The success of the Scandinavian model can be seen in lower reoffending rates compared to other countries. By prioritising rehabilitation and human rights, they have been able to create an environment that encourages personal growth, accountability, and societal reintegration. This approach challenges the traditional punitive model and focuses on providing individuals with the tools and support necessary to break the cycle of crime.

It is important to acknowledge that the Scandinavian model may not be directly applicable to all jurisdictions due to cultural, social, and political differences. However, it serves as a powerful example of how prioritising human rights and rehabilitation can lead to positive outcomes for both prisoners and society as a whole. By studying and adapting successful aspects of this model, other countries can explore ways to improve their own prison systems and work towards a more compassionate and effective approach to incarceration. The SPS has known and visited Scandinavia on many occasions but has implanted zero of the tools used when they come back; the cultural differences are vast, and we must ask ourselves, are we ready for such big changes in the prison system? Are we ready to move away from the punitive approach?

In conclusion, the Scandinavian example highlights the transformative power of prioritising human rights and rehabilitation within the prison system. It demonstrates that punitive approaches alone are insufficient when addressing addiction and trauma, both for prisoners and staff.

Attempting to address complex issues such as addiction and trauma within the confines of a punitive prison setting is an uphill battle. The inherent nature of punishment-focused environments often exacerbates existing problems, perpetuating cycles of reoffending and re-traumatisation. It fails to provide the necessary support and resources for individuals to heal, recover, and reintegrate into society.

For prisoners, punitive approaches can deepen feelings of shame, isolation, and hopelessness, making it challenging for them to address their underlying issues. Moreover, staff members operating within this system face immense difficulties in providing meaningful support due to limited resources, institutional barriers, and a lack of training in addressing complex psychological and social needs.

To effectively address addiction and trauma, it is essential to shift from punitive approaches to ones rooted in compassion, empathy, and rehabilitation. This requires creating environments that prioritise mental health services, evidence-based treatments, and comprehensive support systems for prisoners. It also entails providing staff with the necessary resources, training, and support to effectively engage with and support individuals facing addiction and trauma. Ultimately the government would need to invest to see any improvement, a simple but extremely complex issue when it comes to prison; should it be? I do not know, I would say we need to invest or just own the fact we are warehousing individuals in a toxic and volatile environement, so how can anyone be to blame or at fault, the system or criminal when they reoffend.

Unfortunately we live in a blame culture and personally I believe there are just some things, such as prison and the judiciary that should not be up for sale or debate. It is the role of society to punish and ultimately see fit, to what should be a fitting punishment for a perpetrator of crime. The fact is we should either speak the truth and own the facts of a terrible prison system or stop hiding behind stats and other instruments to sail clear of our blame culture and actually voice what the horrifying reality of these places are.

Acknowledging the limitations of punitive approaches and embracing a more holistic and compassionate paradigm can pave the way for genuine progress. By recognising the humanity of prisoners and the need for trauma-informed care, we can foster environments that promote healing, growth, and successful reintegration into society.

It is time to reimagine our approach to addiction and trauma in prison settings, fostering a culture that supports both prisoners and staff in their journey toward recovery and transformation. By doing so, we can move closer to a system that truly addresses the root causes of crime, promotes rehabilitation, and builds safer and more inclusive communities for all. Cultivating *'authenticity'* in prison would have a multitude of benefits for society as a whole, including:

- **Building Trust:** Authenticity fosters trust among individuals and communities. When people are genuine and true to themselves, it creates a sense of honesty and reliability. This trust is essential for healthy relationships, effective collaboration, and the overall functioning of society.

- **Enhancing Connections:** Authenticity enables deeper connections and understanding between people. When individuals are authentic in their interactions, it allows for genuine communication, empathy, and mutual respect. Authenticity promotes meaningful connections and fosters a sense of belonging within communities.

- **Inspiring Others:** Authenticity serves as an inspiration to others. When individuals openly share their true selves and their unique experiences, it encourages others to embrace their own authenticity. This can lead to personal growth, self-acceptance, and empowerment for individuals who may have felt pressured to conform.

129

- **Promoting Diversity and Inclusion:** Authenticity celebrates diversity and encourages inclusivity. When people are authentic, it creates an environment where different perspectives, identities, and voices are valued and respected. This fosters a society that embraces and appreciates the richness of diversity.

- **Encouraging Innovation and Creativity:** Authenticity is a catalyst for innovation and creativity. When individuals feel free to express their authentic ideas, thoughts, and perspectives, it allows for the emergence of fresh insights and novel solutions to societal challenges. Authenticity sparks creativity and drives positive change.

- **Fostering Well-being:** Authenticity contributes to individual well-being and mental health. When people can be their authentic selves, they experience a sense of self-acceptance, reduced stress, and increased overall happiness. This, in turn, has a positive impact on the well-being of society as a whole.

Overall, authenticity enriches society by cultivating trust, deepening connections, inspiring others, promoting diversity and inclusion, driving innovation, and fostering individual well-being. It creates a more vibrant and harmonious community where people can thrive and contribute their unique talents and perspectives. We can learn from peers who have knowledge to offer and actually try piloting schemes that may well positively change a broken system; instead at the moment we shy away from the truth and for whatever reason hide from the heartbreaking reality in these places.

Chapter Nine: Conquering Castle Huntly: The Ultimate Test

When I finally received acceptance to the Open Estate at HMP Castle Huntly in 2018, a wave of joy washed over me; my good friend James and I were both given the opportunity to go there on the same day, and we couldn't contain our excitement about starting home leaves. We held onto the belief that returning home for a week would be a transformative experience, a chance to escape the confines of our past traumas and find solace in familiar surroundings.

However, the reality proved to be much more complex. Trauma has a way of sticking to us, even when we desperately yearn to shed its weight. It clings to our psyche, infiltrating every aspect of our being. No matter how many physical miles we put between ourselves and the walls that confined us, the emotional and psychological scars remain.

Inside the walls of Castle Huntly, amidst the stories and experiences shared by fellow inmates, the trauma echoed and reverberated. The atmosphere was heavy with the weight of past pain and the struggle to overcome it. The hypocrisy we encountered only added to the burden, a stark reminder that healing and redemption are not easily achieved within the confines of a system that is itself plagued by contradictions.

To describe the experience as merely unpleasant falls short of capturing the depth of its impact. It was a visceral reminder that trauma, once imprinted upon our souls, is not easily erased. It lingers, seeping into our thoughts, emotions, and relationships. It is a constant companion, reminding us of our past, shaping our present, and influencing our future.

Authenticity in chaos

Yet, despite the enduring nature of trauma, there is hope. It lies in acknowledging its presence, seeking support, and nurturing resilience. It lies in recognizing that healing is a journey, and though the path may be arduous, it is not insurmountable. However, Castle Huntly is not a place that cultivates this kind of trauma-informed practice, that is needed when you are starting to reintegrate back into society.

So, the SPS motto is **"unlocking potential and transforming lives."** While I can agree with the notion of transforming lives, I must argue that the impact at HMP Castle Huntly is far from the positive transformation they would have you believe. Located in the breathtaking surroundings of Longforgan, Dundee, this prison boasts impressive views that can easily deceive visitors and government officials into thinking it is a well-maintained environment, instead of well-maintained grounds; that you cannot argue with.

However, the truth of prison life within these walls is a completely different story. Here lies the tricky part: Castle Huntly is a facade, a grand illusion where everyone plays a game of "unauthenticity" in order to survive. Behind the seemingly idyllic exterior, a dark undercurrent prevails. Drug abuse runs rampant, bullying thrives, staff intimidation persists, power imbalances persist, and a state of hypervigilance permeates the atmosphere like no other place I've experienced before.

In this environment, authenticity becomes a luxury that few can afford. It becomes a challenge to remain true to oneself amidst the constant pressures and manipulations. To navigate the intricacies of this hidden world, individuals often find themselves adopting personas, concealing their vulnerabilities, and playing the roles required to endure.

The transformation happening within these walls is not one of positive growth or redemption. It is a transformation forced upon individuals, molding them into something unrecognisable from their authentic selves. The toll it takes on mental and emotional well-being is immeasurable.

The transition to Castle Huntly is vastly different from moving to a mainstream prison. Although it offers more freedom, this newfound liberty comes with a constant reminder that it could be taken away at any moment, often for seemingly minor reasons, such as associating with the wrong crowd. The very existence of a "wrong crowd" within Castle Huntly is intriguing in itself.

The process to reach the open estate is incredibly intricate and exhaustive. Approval is required from both prison-based social workers and community social workers to be considered for the open estate. Moreover, the governor must deem you as low-risk, and all the staff, including those who worked with you through relevant coursework, must also acknowledge your low-risk status. It's an incredibly stringent process that one must go through before being granted access to Castle Huntly.

In theory, once you've arrived at Castle Huntly, there should be no reason to steer clear of anyone or fear potential downgrades, as everyone has undergone the same rigorous vetting process. It becomes nonsensical and baffling when the threat of downgrade arises due to the staff's perception of risky associations. How can this be justified, given the thoroughness of the selection process? The paradoxical situation defies logic.

Castle Huntly, much like top-end prisons, exhibits an alarmingly low success rate, particularly for those who have served lengthy sentences. While some caring staff members genuinely attempt to aid in the process and overlook minor setbacks, others relish their power and create additional hurdles, adding to the already overwhelming stress of the experience. A typical day at Castle Huntly involves engaging in various prison work parties, be it in the kitchen or as passmen, but there are also outside placements for those who opt for such opportunities.

These placements can range from working in charity shops to volunteering at third-sector organizations. I was fortunate with my own placement, as I got to work with vulnerable individuals and help them lead better lives. Such charities can be a lifeline for some, but sadly, not all placements are as rewarding. Many placements resemble slave labor, and despite the kindness of the people running them, there's a lingering feeling that they view prisoners as mere free labor.

In reality, these placements fail to prepare individuals for a successful reintegration into society. The evening classes, though poorly attended, aim to teach life skills, computer literacy, and money management. Yet, the power imbalance and unjust resume loom over the process, with the incentive of a week out each month serving as the carrot.

Home leaves are undeniably amazing, but what I observed and heard from most individuals in Castle Huntly was that the lifestyle experienced there was far from realistic. It felt more like a holiday than a genuine attempt at reintegrating into the community. Despite this apparent disconnection from reality, I recognize the importance of even this idealized way of living, as it is vital for anyone who has served a long sentence to stand a chance of success upon release.

In my perspective, Castle Huntly is a place where authenticity is at its lowest. You find yourself playing the role of the prisoner inside the prison, the prisoner at your placement, and the prisoner for your loved ones on the outside. This constant juggling of different personas is an incredibly challenging way to live, and it may shed light on why drug use becomes such a prevalent issue in the open estate. Trying to divide your personality into multiple pieces takes a toll, especially when you're well aware that one minor misstep could send you back to closed conditions for a significant period, perhaps even a year.

Improving authenticity in an open estate is a complex dilemma with no easy answers. From my own experience, I can confidently say that Castle Huntly presents the most formidable test of them all. The pressure to maintain a facade and conform to different expectations can be overwhelming, leading to a struggle for one's true self to emerge amidst the complex dynamics of the open estate.

Improving authenticity in the open estate is a multi-faceted challenge that requires a comprehensive approach. There is already some stuff in place, but I would concentrate on:

- **Therapeutic Programs:** Implement tailored therapeutic programs that focus on self-discovery, emotional expression, and personal growth. These programs could include counseling, group therapy, and workshops designed to encourage self-reflection and building genuine connections.

- **Mental Health Support:** Prioritise mental health support for inmates. Offer regular counseling sessions and access to mental health professionals who can help individuals cope with the pressures of maintaining multiple personas.

- **Holistic Reintegration Approach:** Develop a holistic reintegration approach that considers the individual's background, interests, and skills. Tailor their prison work placements to align with their strengths and interests, which can foster a sense of identity and authenticity.

- **Family and Community Involvement:** Facilitate meaningful family and community involvement in the reintegration process. Encourage open communication between inmates and their loved ones to build authentic relationships and support systems.

- **Vocational Training:** Provide comprehensive vocational training and education to enhance inmates' employability upon release. Fostering skills and knowledge in a field of interest can instill a sense of purpose and authenticity.

- **Peer Support Groups:** Establish peer support groups within the open estate where inmates can openly discuss their struggles and experiences. This can create a sense of belonging and provide a safe space for authentic self-expression.

- **Conflict Resolution Training:** Offer conflict resolution training to teach inmates constructive ways to navigate disagreements and handle interpersonal challenges without resorting to violence or manipulation.

- **Reducing Stigmatisation:** Work towards reducing the stigma associated with being an ex-offender. Promote understanding and empathy in society to encourage a more inclusive and supportive environment for successful reintegration. Invite members of the community around Castle Huntly to come in and see prisoners and have a chat with some of them.

- **Aftercare Programs:** Develop comprehensive aftercare programs that continue to support individuals after their release. Provide access to community resources, mentors, and support networks to help former inmates sustain their authentic selves in the outside world.

- **Regular Evaluations:** Conduct regular evaluations of the effectiveness of authenticity-focused initiatives in the open estate. Use feedback from inmates and staff to refine and improve the programs over time.

Addressing authenticity in the open estate requires a shift from punitive measures to a rehabilitative and empathetic approach. By providing the necessary support, opportunities, and resources, we can empower individuals to discover and embrace their authentic selves, leading to a more successful and fulfilling reintegration into society. In fairness, I have seen the staff at Castle Huntly try out these kinds of projects, but for either security issues or lack of interest, they fall away. So, how do we muster up interest in this kind of approach?

Engaging individuals in Castle Huntly and making participation more appealing can be achieved through a combination of approaches that focus on intrinsic motivation and providing meaningful incentives. Here are some ideas:

- **Choice and Autonomy:** Offer a variety of programs and activities that cater to different interests and talents. Allowing inmates to choose activities that resonate with them will make participation more voluntary and enjoyable.

- **Relevance and Practicality:** Ensure that programs are relevant to their post-release goals and practical in everyday life. Demonstrating how acquired skills can be useful outside of the prison environment can increase interest and motivation.

- **Peer Involvement:** Encourage inmates who have benefited from certain programs to share their success stories and experiences with others. Peer testimonials can inspire engagement and foster a sense of camaraderie.

- **Positive Reinforcement:** Implement a system of positive reinforcement, such as recognition and rewards for active participation. Acknowledge progress, achievements, and efforts to make the experience more fulfilling.

- **Meaningful Certifications:** Offer certifications or qualifications for completing certain programs. These credentials can boost self-esteem and employability prospects, providing a tangible incentive for engagement.

- **Family Involvement:** Facilitate family involvement and support in programs. Organize family days or events where inmates can showcase their progress, fostering a sense of pride and encouragement from loved ones.

- **Recreational and Creative Activities:** Introduce recreational and creative activities that promote self-expression and stress relief. Art, music, sports, and writing workshops can offer enjoyable outlets and encourage participation.

- **Personal Development Focus:** Emphasise personal development and growth rather than just compliance with rules. Encourage self-awareness, emotional intelligence, and empathy to foster a sense of purpose and authenticity.

- **Community Impact:** Link programs to community service projects where inmates can positively contribute and witness the impact of their efforts. Knowing that they can make a difference may boost engagement.

- **Incentive-based Initiatives:** Consider offering incentives like reduced sentences or earlier eligibility for certain privileges based on active participation and positive behavioral changes.

- **Continuous Feedback and Improvement:** Regularly seek feedback from inmates about the programs and activities. Use their input to adapt and improve offerings to better align with their interests and needs.

The illogical issue I observed in the open estate is the practice of making everyone pay for the mistakes of one individual. A glaring example of this was the running club, a beneficial initiative that promoted fitness and mental well-being by getting individuals to run a few nights a week. Unfortunately, one person made a poor decision to meet their partner during the route, resulting in the entire project being shut down. The same pattern occurred with other projects, such as the fishing and hillwalking programs. It's understandable to address security concerns and take necessary precautions, but it's unfair and unjust to penalise the entire prison population for the actions of a single individual. A more rational approach would involve tightening security measures without depriving the entire community of the valuable opportunities these projects provide.

We could make the open estate a much more enjoyable and productive stage of an individual sentence by drawing inspiration from successful initiatives in other countries, such as Norway's respect-based approach, Germany's emphasis on vocational training, and New Zealand's restorative justice programs, we can build a more compassionate and effective open estate system that empowers inmates to grow, learn, and successfully reintegrate into society. There are different approaches to open estates around the world, and we could learn a lot from taking some of the good from each and coming up with our own, giving the individual back some 'authenticity' instead of unknowingly encouraging our prisoners to be unauthentic and hindering their chances of success on the outside. Here are just some ways that other countries do things again. This could be a societal matter and just may be the fact that the UK is not ready for such radical change to our prison system:

Norway's Open Prison System:

Norway is renowned for its humane and effective approach to incarceration. Its open prison system emphasizes rehabilitation and reintegration, with an emphasis on trust and individual responsibility. In open prisons like Bastoy, inmates live in small houses or cottages, enjoying greater freedom and autonomy compared to traditional prisons. They have access to vocational training, educational programs, and work opportunities that align with their interests and skills. Inmates actively participate in daily chores and decision-making processes, promoting a sense of ownership and accountability. The open prison system in Norway has shown impressive results, with lower reoffending rates compared to traditional prisons.

Germany's Open Prison Programs:

Germany has a successful approach to open prisons that focuses on vocational training and education. Inmates in open prisons have the opportunity to work in various fields, gaining valuable skills and work experience that enhance their employability post-release. One example is the Berlin Open Prison, where inmates can work in carpentry, metalworking, gardening, and other trades. The emphasis on vocational training helps inmates reintegrate into society as productive and self-sufficient individuals, reducing the likelihood of reoffending.

Finland's Open Prisons:

Finland's open prison system is centered on the concept of trust and personal responsibility. Inmates in open prisons have greater freedom of movement within the prison grounds and may have access to external work or educational opportunities. For instance, the Hämeenlinna Open Prison allows inmates to work in nearby farms and businesses, fostering a sense of purpose and connection to the outside world. The emphasis on trust and responsibility helps inmates develop a sense of self-discipline and accountability, contributing to their successful reintegration.

Australia's Low-Security Correctional Facilities:

In Australia, there are various low-security correctional facilities that operate similarly to open prisons. These facilities aim to prepare inmates for their eventual release by providing access to education, vocational training, and therapeutic programs. The emphasis is on rehabilitation, with a focus on addressing underlying issues such as substance abuse and mental health. Inmates in these low-security facilities are more likely to participate in community work projects, gaining a sense of responsibility and connection to society.

Sweden's Open Prison Model:

Sweden's open prison model allows inmates to work outside the prison during the day, returning to the facility in the evenings. The focus is on gradually reintegrating inmates into society, promoting their responsibility and independence. The opportunity to work and interact with the community allows inmates to gain valuable life skills and build positive relationships, contributing to their successful transition back into society.

The reason I looked into the above countries is they seem to have a better success rate than Scotland. This may be due to societal and cultural differences, but I think it is all about empowering the individual to go back into the community with self-esteem and confidence in a way that will allow the individual to become a part of the community they go back to and be allowed to move on from the inhumane conditions and treatment that they have been privy to for many years. Surely, we can take the best parts of each country and look to try and implement them into our open estate so we are not churning out hypervigilant and traumatized individuals and then demonizing them as soon as they step a foot wrong. I understand from the victim's view as well that for some crimes like murder, rape, etc. that they believe the individuals accountable for these crimes should not be given another chance, this is quite natural to feel like this, and to be honest, I do not know how we counteract that mindset, as many families have gone through great heartbreak and turmoil.

In the Scottish system, it is a reality that offenders will eventually be released. Therefore, it is crucial to focus on positively rehabilitating prisoners to reduce the risk of future harm to society. While this approach may provide an opportunity for offenders to lead better lives, it can be disheartening for victims who may feel let down by the system. In such circumstances, there are no true winners, and both parties may harbor feelings of disappointment. The Scottish Prison Service's promotion and boast of rehabilitation may seem misleading, as the actual efforts toward this goal appear limited. This lack of effective rehabilitation increases the likelihood of future victims being affected by the same individuals who were let down during their time in incarceration. It is essential to acknowledge and address the issues of hopelessness, addiction, mental health problems, and other negative consequences prevalent within prisons. By openly recognizing these challenges, society can work towards crafting a more effective system that genuinely supports individuals going through the judicial process, ensuring a safer and more positive environment for everyone involved.

As this chapter draws to a close, it becomes evident that mental health issues, addiction, and a pervasive sense of low self-worth are often byproducts of attempting to maintain authenticity in an unauthentic environment. Anxiety, depression, disassociation, PTSD, and unresolved childhood trauma are just a few examples of the challenges that arise when individuals find themselves disconnected from their true selves. Navigating the minefield of authenticity in such a cruel and unauthentic setting poses a daunting dilemma. Should one simply accept the prevailing circumstances as they are, choosing to harden up and conform to the world's ways? Or are these issues more profound, exerting a genuine impact on our mental psyche?

As we reflect on these questions, it becomes clear that authenticity in an unauthentic environment is an arduous journey. The pressure to conform to societal norms, the struggle to reconcile one's values with the prevailing system, and the harsh consequences of deviating from the established norms all contribute to a profound sense of disconnection and internal conflict. The desire to be true to oneself becomes entangled with the need to survive within the confines of an unauthentic reality.

Within this complex web, mental health issues and addiction often emerge as coping mechanisms or responses to the stress of this incongruity. Suppressing one's authentic self can lead to a range of emotional and psychological struggles, resulting in anxiety, depression, and other mental health challenges. The traumatic experiences that led to this disconnect, such as childhood trauma, may further exacerbate these issues.

Authenticity in chaos

The journey towards authenticity demands not only personal resilience but also systemic change. Recognizing the impact of unauthentic environments on mental well-being calls for a compassionate and empathetic approach to rehabilitation and reintegration. Addressing mental health issues, addiction, and low self-worth requires a comprehensive system that emphasizes mental health support, counseling, and trauma-informed care.

Ultimately, it is essential to confront the tension between authenticity and an unauthentic world. By fostering a culture that values individual growth, personal expression, and genuine connection, we can begin to create environments that allow for true authenticity to flourish. Only then can we hope to diminish the harmful effects on our mental psyche, supporting individuals in reclaiming their true selves and finding solace amidst the turbulence of an unauthentic reality.

Chapter Ten: Navigating the Path Forward

As we conclude this journey through the intricacies of the prison system, it becomes increasingly evident that the current trajectory is far from sustainable. The issues we've explored, from the struggles of authenticity within the prison walls to the challenges of rehabilitation and the impact on mental health, paint a sobering picture of a system in dire need of reevaluation.

A Glimpse at the Stats:

Let's face the facts: the statistics don't lie. The current approach to incarceration, rehabilitation, and reintegration is not yielding the results we need. Recidivism rates remain high, mental health challenges persist, and drug trends within the prison walls mirror a broader societal crisis. It's not just an isolated problem; it's a reflection of deeper issues that demand our attention.

The Unsettling Drug Trends:

A stark reality that cannot be ignored is the prevailing drug epidemic within the prison system. Drug abuse is not only a consequence of unauthentic environments but also a symptom of a system ill-equipped to address the root causes. The trend is troubling, and it signals a need for a more empathetic and effective approach to tackling addiction and its underlying triggers.

The Urgent Call for Empathy:

It's time for a paradigm shift. We stand at a crossroads where the path we choose will determine the future of our society. Continuing on the current trajectory will only perpetuate a cycle of despair, fostering hypervigilance, trauma, and disconnection. The key to breaking this cycle lies in empathy—on both sides of the prison walls.

Empathy in Action:

Empathy is not just a buzzword; it's the cornerstone of a compassionate and effective prison system. It starts with acknowledging the humanity of individuals within the system, recognizing that everyone has a story and the potential for change. From prison staff to policymakers, from victims to offenders, fostering empathy can bridge the gap and pave the way for genuine rehabilitation.

Bridging the Gap:

To bridge this gap, we must revisit and revamp the system. It requires a multi-faceted approach that prioritizes mental health support, personalized rehabilitation programs, and opportunities for skill development. The focus should shift from punishment to understanding, from isolation to connection.

A Glimpse into a More Empathetic Future:

Looking ahead, we find inspiration in countries that have reimagined their prison systems. Norway's respect-based approach, Germany's emphasis on vocational training, and Finland's trust-centered model offer glimpses into a future where empathy is not just a goal but a reality.

The Power of Change:

Change is never easy, but it is necessary. By embracing empathy, we can create an environment where authenticity is not a luxury but a fundamental right. It's about recognizing that everyone, regardless of their past, deserves a chance at redemption, growth, and reintegration into society.

The Call to Action:

As we close this chapter, let it be a call to action. A plea to policymakers, prison staff, communities, and individuals alike to champion a more empathetic and effective prison system. It's an invitation to break free from the shackles of an outdated approach and build a future where authenticity, mental health, and rehabilitation are at the forefront.

In layman's terms, it's time to treat individuals within the system with the humanity they deserve. It's about understanding that change is possible, but it requires a system that nurtures growth rather than perpetuates despair. The path forward is clear: empathy, understanding, and a collective commitment to building a future where the prison system is not a cycle of degradation but a path toward redemption and reconnection.

Because, let's be brutally honest, in the current conditions, being your authentic self within the confines of the prison system is akin to navigating a labyrinth with walls that seem to close in at every turn. The struggle for authenticity becomes a formidable challenge, weighed down by the pressures of conformity, the scars of past traumas, and the ever-present threat of danger and judgment.

Yet, in recognising the near impossibility of authenticity, we unveil an urgent truth: the system needs restructuring. The realisation that individuals find it nearly impossible to be their authentic selves within the existing framework serves as a poignant call for reform. It demands a collective effort to dismantle the barriers that hinder personal growth, perpetuates trauma, and obscure the path to redemption.

As we contemplate the road ahead, let us not forget the power of empathy and the potential for change. A future where authenticity thrives within the prison system is not an unattainable ideal but a necessary evolution. By embracing empathy, understanding, and a commitment to reshaping the system, we can pave the way for a prison environment that empowers individuals to reclaim their true selves.

If we lay the foundation for a future where authenticity is not just a dream but a reality—one that transcends the limitations of the present and illuminates a path toward a more humane and compassionate prison system, we help not just prisoners but help by creating potential future victims of crime.

In closing, this work is dedicated to all those confined behind the steel bars and invisible walls of the prison system. To every individual who has grappled with the struggle for authenticity within an environment that often seems designed to suppress it, your resilience does not go unnoticed. May this dedication stand as a testament to your strength and as a reminder that, even in the face of adversity, the flame of hope can endure.

This dedication extends equally to the dedicated individuals working within the system, ensnared in the labyrinth of bureaucracy and red tape. Your efforts, often constrained by institutional constraints, bureaucratic hurdles, and systemic challenges, do not go unappreciated. May this serve as recognition for your commitment to the betterment of those within your care and for your endurance amid the complexities of the system.

May this work inspire a collective call for reform, empathy, and understanding, fostering an environment where both those incarcerated and those working within the system find a pathway toward healing and transformation. In the spirit of shared humanity, may we collectively strive for a future that values authenticity, compassion, and the potential for redemption within the prison system. I truly hope one day we create a system that as a society we can be proud of.

Acknowledgments

As I reflect upon the completion of my inaugural literary endeavor, I am compelled to express my deepest gratitude to the remarkable individuals who have played an instrumental role in bringing this book to fruition.

Foremost, heartfelt thanks extend to Fiona whom I love dearly, my cherished mother and father. Their unwavering guidance, though occasionally adorned with suggestions that tested my patience, has been an indispensable compass throughout this creative journey. To my steadfast siblings, Barry and Eilish, whose unwavering support served as a pillar of strength during the arduous writing process, I am truly grateful.

I am indebted to the invaluable contributions of Scott Jenkins and the entire MOJO team, Natalie Logan, Becky Hall, Julie Thomson, James Docherty, Laura Ferguson, Cary Griffen, the entire Loves and Griffens clans, Andrew, and all those who took the time to delve into the pages of my work, providing invaluable feedback. Your collective engagement has enriched the tapestry of my storytelling.

Special appreciation goes to Ross Kelter, whose unyielding belief in my abilities served as a beacon of encouragement, and to David Smith, whose substantial assistance significantly contributed to the realization of this literary endeavor. To all my friends who have been there for me, again, too many to mention but thanks to you all.

In closing, I dedicate this book to the memory of those who have left an indelible mark on my life, particularly my dear Granny Mary and Granny Sadie, Granda Joe my uncle Tam, and Don who all sadly passed away whilst I was in prison. To all my family who have supported me, too many to mention but I love you all and will never forget the support. A heartfelt tribute is extended to all the prisoners who faced their struggles, with a special mention to Ryan, whose journey toward brighter horizons inspires hope. To the countless others behind prison walls who stood by me, your camaraderie is acknowledged with profound gratitude.

As I embark on this literary odyssey, I eagerly anticipate the prospect of weaving more tales in the future. The road ahead beckons with promise, and I am grateful for the encouragement and support that has paved the way for this inaugural endeavor.

Bibliography

Works Cited

Guillemets, Terri. The Quote Garden, Retrieved 2023

Kabat Zin, Jon. "Jon Kabat-Zinn Quotes." BrainyQuote. Xplore. Web., Retrieved 2023

Musk, Elon. BrainyQuote. (n.d.). Elon Musk Quotes. Retrieved 2023

Mate, Gabor. "Choosing Between Authenticity and Attachment." Psychology Today. Sussex Publishers. Web. 2023

Brown, Brene. Authenticity is a collection of choices." Brené Brown. Web. Retrieved 2023

Sadghuru. "Sadhguru Quotes." The Yogi Press. Web. 2023

Machiavelli, Niccolo. "Niccolò Machiavelli Quotes." Goodreads. Web. 2023

Covey. Stephen. Stephen Covey Quotes About Self Awareness." A-Z Quotes. Web. 2023

Buddha. Gautama. BrainyQuote. (n.d.). Gautama Buddha Quotes. Retrieved 2023

Lama. Dalai. Psychology Today. (n.d.). Dalai Lama Quotes. Retrieved 2023

Gibson. Andrea. Andrea Gibson Quotes." Goodreads. Web Retrieved 2023

Krishnamurti, Jiddu. Jiddu Krishnamurti Quotes." Wildmind. Web. 2023

Mate Gabor. Gabor Maté Quotes." Goodreads. Web. 2023

"Table with Motto." SPS Website. Web. 2023

Zimbardo, P. (1971). Stanford Prison Experiment. <u>Retrieved 2023, from Stanford University</u>[1]

"Exclusive: Convicts riot in luxury Addiewell Prison eight weeks after it opens" – Daily Record, Web. 2023

"IN THE NICK OF TIME Tough Scots prison ranked as second cushiest in the WORLD for cons" – The Sun, Web. 2023

"Britain's LUXURY prisons: Inside the jails where lags live like kings" – Daily Star, Web. 2023

"Prisoners." Judge Dennis A. Challeen. Web. 2023

Tutu. Desmond. Desmond Tutu Quotes. Goodreads. Web. 2023

Luther King Jr. Martin. "Martin Luther King Jr. Quotes." The Guardian. Web. 2023

Churchill. Winston. "Winston Churchill Quotes." BrainyQuote. Xplore. Web. 2023

Einstein, A. (n.d.). In Goodreads. Retrieved December 16, 2023,

Chomsky. Noam. Noam Chomsky Quotes. (n.d.). In A-Z Quotes. Retrieved 2023.

Thompson, H. S. (n.d.). In Goodreads. Retrieved 2023

Coelho, P. (n.d.). In Goodreads. Retrieved 2023

Frank, A. (n.d.). In Goodreads. Retrieved 2023

Authenticity in chaos
Roosevelt, D F. Radio Address for the Mobilization for Human Needs. (n.d.). In The American Presidency Project. Retrieved 2023

Gandhi, M. (n.d.). In Goodreads. Retrieved 2023

Canfield. J. (n.d) in Goodreads. Retrieved 2023

Printed in Great Britain
by Amazon